Moments in Transition
Stories of Maya and Jeena

Moments in Transition
Stories of Maya and Jeena

NEERJA RAMAN

ISBN: 1976218578
ISBN-13: 9781976218576

Also by Neerja Raman

The Practice and Philosophy of Decision Making: A Seven Step Spiritual Guide

To my husband, Vasan, and our kids—Kavita, Priya, and Arjun—who grew up when I blinked.

With Much Love

One day I will find the right words
and they will be simple.

—JACK KEROUAC

CONTENTS

Preface   xiii
Acknowledgments   xv
Endorsements   xvii
Author's Note   xxv

1	Once Upon a River	1
2	Closet Communications	10
3	The House on Cantonment Road	14
4	Color Me Happy	19
5	Maya's Mantra	22
6	My Dad and the Duchess	32
7	Uptown Girl	35
8	A Cup of Restraint	44
9	Underneath the Guava Tree	47
10	Bread, Book, and Candle	52
11	National Highway 8 to Delhi	58
12	Fearless Feet	67
13	The Intruder on Our Balcony	74
14	One Evening in the Park	79
15	The Bug Affair	87
16	Margarita Love	91
17	My First Friend	96
18	A Walk in the Wetlands	100
19	The Open Door	103
20	When Moms Grow Up	111

21   Garden of People   117
22   Tradition   125

Glossary   129
About the Author   133

PREFACE

The sun shines,
And the flowers bloom.

When I am sad
And I am blue,

I remind myself
To do what I must do.

The heavens pour, the rivers gurgle,
And the mountains beckon.

When I am happy,
and I am true,

I ask myself, "What do I dream?"
Then I do what I think I cannot do.

ACKNOWLEDGMENTS

Many thanks to all who've read and commented on stories in this novel. Thanks to Bonnie Bolling, Matty Byloos, Rebecca Leboeuf, Jaya Padmanabhan, Nirupama Vaidhyanathan, and David Walker for support and encouragement.

Some stories previously appeared in same or slightly different form in *Golden Walkman* ("Uptown Girl"), *India Currents* ("Fearless Feet" and "Garden of People"), *Nailed Magazine* ("Margarita Love"), *Penmen Review* ("Once Upon a River"), and *Verdad* ("Once Upon a River"). In 2017 Katha Contest, the short story "Garden of People" won honorable mention, with Steve Kettmann and Sarah Ringler of the Wellstone Center as judges.

I am grateful to Sylvia Halloran for insightful advice on cross cultural themes and to Sharon Bray, whose creative writing class inspired this journey.

ENDORSEMENTS

Neerja Raman is a very creative writer. Her stories have heart as well as humor.

—**Deepka Lalwani**, founder Indian Business & Professional Women, advisor SiliconValleyReads.org, Intero realtor

Neerja Raman uses eloquent vocabulary and expression to make a personal connection with her reader. "Once Upon a River" evoked the same feelings in me as Jeena; as if they belong to me as well.

—**Manjula Pal**, *Freelance Journalist*, India

Excellent. I have read three short stories and enjoyed each one. Looking forward to the book.

—**Lalita Chadha**, retired professor, Daulat Ram College, India

Comments on Individual stories:

When Moms Grow Up

> Neerja, you are a gifted writer, expressing deep emotion and insight in a way that conveys that you are talking directly to me as your reader.

—**Betty Sproule**, author of *The Stuff Cure: How We Lost 8,000 Pounds of Stuff for Fun, Profit, Virtue, and a Better World*

> Brought tears. Really like the concept, "Moms who make the hard choices and mothers who have hard choices made for them." Your words conjure clear images.

—**Kalpana Shyam**, Senior Software Engineer, IBM

> Deeply moving and so true.

—**Smita Deshpande**, marketing, author at "Network Virtualization," a VMware blog

Garden of People

Neerja Raman, what a wonderful story! It's deep on many levels. A winner for sure. It made me cry, reminding me of similar lessons from my own father.

—**Barbara Waugh,** author of *The Soul in the Computer: The Story of a Corporate Revolutionary* and executive in residence at Haas School of Business, UC Berkeley

Beautiful, Neerja. I love the way you connect the past to the present. My father also left a deep impression on me.

—**Rudite Emir**, California

"My garden of people will prosper if I express love, understanding, and trust...I must cultivate this garden." Beautifully said, Neerja Raman. We all need to do that. Always, always.

—**Neelima Garg**, schoolteacher, California

Once Upon a River

Beautifully written and strikes a chord. I loved it.

—**Radha Penekelapati**, technical professional at Google

The story has so creatively explained fervent yet tender emotions circling around the rituals emerging into peace and solitude. I read it a few times to sip in the depth of it.

—**Matra Mazumdar**, yoga and nutrition coach, SACHI board member

Very nice. I could relate to your writing as Varanasi River, and all that happens there is close to my heart!

—**Latika Sharma Katt**, sculptor, art teacher, and winner of 4th Beijing Biennale Award (2010)

A very nice short story. Quite evocative. Getting rid of emotional baggage, atonement, and unblocking of the heart. Great theme and nicely narrated. Hope one can learn from Jeena's story and let love flow even before one loses one's dear ones.

—**Ashok Vaish**, entrepreneur and venture investor in the Silicon Valley and blogger, "The Capitalist Muse: A Blog about Money Matters and What Matters"

Beautiful. Touching. Magic.

—**Deb Colden**, executive coaching and strategy facilitation

I really liked "Once Upon a River." Very well written, and Neerja Raman has done such a good job describing some very complex emotions.

—**Sheila Mohan**, finance professional, California

I loved this one. Very talented and inspiring!

—**Gayathri Sreekanth**, Edmonton, Alberta

The Intruder on Our Balcony

It is a sweet little story. The descriptions are very vivid, and I can see the two pigeons right in front of my eyes. I will look at these pests who come to roost in our balconies in India through a different eye now.

—**Poornima Kumar**, biochemist

Uptown Girl

I like the title; it got my attention. A good story that keeps you wondering as to what is going to happen to Jeena. Will she get attacked or will she escape or is there a 3rd outcome? Had a message as well regarding Jeena building her confidence in getting out of a scary situation and surprising herself.

—**Kalpana Shyam,** Senior Software Engineer, IBM

Tradition

I love every word that you have written and expressed here and can relate, having shared the same growing-up environment.

—**Alok Chandola**, Higher! Realms, India

I particularly liked how you created the image of your current attendance and your attendance as a girl.

—**Betty Sproule**, author of *The Stuff Cure: How We Lost 8,000 Pounds of Stuff for Fun, Profit, Virtue, and a Better World*

AUTHOR'S NOTE

My father told bedtime stories with a glint in his eye that belied the grin on his face. When he stopped, we chorused, "And the moral of the story is…greed leads to grief, ego leads to fall, fighting leads to loss…" And so on.

But not always. One story he loved to confound us with is "Two Cats":

> *A big cat saw a little cat chasing its tail and asked, "Why are you chasing your tail so?"*
>
> *"I have heard that the best thing for a cat is happiness, and that happiness is in my tail. Therefore, I am chasing my tail, and when I catch it, I will have happiness."*
>
> *Said the old cat, "My child, I too have paid attention to the problems of the universe. I too have judged that happiness is in my tail. But I have noticed that, when I chase my tail, it runs away from me. And when I go about my business, it just seems to come after me wherever I go."*

At that time, I thought I was the little cat. I grew up, and then I was the big cat. Now I am both cats, sometimes at the same moment in time.

The water is cooler than she expected. Yet it warms her too. While it looked muddy from the boat, here down below the water is clear. Jeena opens her eyes and looks around. She sees her sari billow about in the water, caressing her legs. Slowly she begins to feel the embrace of the shadows playing around her.

Then suddenly she panics. She bobs back up to look at the boatman. "It's cold."

He nods and waves her away. Taking a deep breath, she dips her head in underwater and counts to ten before swimming out, farther away from the boat, still clutching the urn in her arms.

This time Jeena is more relaxed, and she feels the gentleness that lies within the powerful currents. She opens her heart until finally her tears start to flow. She uncorks the urn and tilts it upside down to see ashes float around. She sees her tears mix with the ashes to form an embrace. Mother Ganga has taken her back into the shelter of her womb. Her words and her sorrow dissolve in the purity of her mother's soul. It cleanses and heals, and once done, it opens its arms, birthing her anew.

Fifteen minutes later, minus the urn and ashes and the sari clinging wet, Jeena swims back to the boat and climbs in. Without breaking the spell, the boatman rows her back to the ghat. A newborn Jeena is wrapped in an embrace that will never go away.

Next morning, like any other tourist, Jeena packs her bags and hails a taxi to catch her flight back home. But she no longer looks at the taxi driver with suspicion when she pays the fare. She waits patiently in line to get to her seat. After takeoff, she takes her first deep breath in six days. She notices her lungs inflate with ease. There is no constriction in her heart. Her hands relax in her lap.

Having forgiven herself, Jeena can now forgive others. She is gentler, kinder, and wiser. A smile plays on her face. Even before the plane has reached cruising altitude, Jeena falls asleep.

The river has done her duty.

2

CLOSET COMMUNICATIONS

The Bungalow is more than a home style, it's a lifestyle.

The Bungalow Company (https://
thebungalowcompany.com/bungalow-lifestyle/)

When Jerald and Maya went looking for a house to buy in
suburban San Francisco, the first thing Maya inspected were
the closets.

And she would laugh. "You call this a closet? This is not a
closet! Not even close!"

"What's wrong with the closet? That's how closets are in
America," Jerald would say.

Maya grew up in India in a large, rather rambling house
with interconnected rooms where not only her mother, father, sister, the dog, and various service personnel ran about

unconstrained, but also an odd visitor or two was known to have been spotted.

Maya's favorite place in that house was the closet. Besides being a place to change clothes, it was her hiding spot, along with her safe place and private thinking room. It was a place to get away when life was confusing.

And all this was possible because the closet in her house was not a closet at all but a small room with a solid wooden door that could be locked from the inside. In contrast to the chaos of the house, the closet was predictable, where at one glance Maya could tell if all were right with her world...or not.

"The closet is barely big enough for clothes, Jerald. If something were to happen, how would I know?"

"What does a closet have to do with knowing what's going on?"

"Everything. That's how I know what to do."

Maya's house, as typical of bungalow architecture, did not have the American-style closet. Instead her mother had designated a small room in their house to function as the family closet. A multipurpose space, it was equipped with a square corner table where clothes could be piled on for ironing. One wall was hidden behind a large steel almirah style wardrobe, which could be locked (but almost never was) for jewelry, money, expensive saris, and her father's suits. Open shelves lined two other walls. Pegs for hanging clothes were installed at different heights and in the middle.

There was a small area where Maya stood to get dressed. Clothes for the whole week were stocked for the family in their individually allotted spaces. Every Sunday, dirty laundry disappeared, and Maya's shelf was restocked with clean, starched school uniforms, fresh pajamas, socks, underwear, and evening frocks.

Every weekday morning after her shower, Maya would run into the closet, change into her school uniform, dart out for breakfast, and head off to school. The process was reversed in the evening: come back from school, place uniform in the dirty laundry basket, change into frock, and head off to play. And then at night, she changed into pajamas.

Everyone knew, if the closet door were closed, it meant the person inside wanted privacy, usually to change from one outfit into another, and so he or she was left alone. The closet was a place of order and structure in an otherwise independent household. Its space was how they communicated. A change in its order was significant. There were the little things. If laundry were not cleared, it meant there was friction with the washerwoman, Mother would be rushed, and it was best to pretend not to notice. If the almirah door stood ajar, Mother and Father had an evening out.

Maya's parents tacked notes on the closet walls to let each other and even Maya and her sister know of a change in the daily routine.

And then there were the big things. Soft sobbing noises sometimes came from the closet, along with shouting and bickering when Father was on a rampage. And even absolute quiet, without any shuffling and swooshing of clothes, portended an ill wind.

"Without a proper closet, how do I get some privacy?"

"What privacy? A closet is for clothes, not privacy."

"We all need private time," Maya would say and land a peck on Jerald's cheek.

And so it was that Maya's first adjustment in America had more to do with architecture than anything else.

Communication was not the problem, said Maya, but houses having separate rooms connected via a corridor led to a needless custom of isolation in America. A small closet good enough only for hanging clothes meant a whole room was needed for privacy. And where was the sense in that?

3

THE HOUSE ON CANTONMENT ROAD

From a security point of view, the house Papa, my father, moved us into was considered undesirable. As a routine matter, it was allocated to new incoming schoolmasters with the understanding that a few years later, when another master was hired, they could trade up and vacate the house for the new recruit to occupy. So when Papa accepted the new job, there was no other choice. We moved.

"How can we live in this house?" my mother Amma objected when she saw where it was located.

"It is a fine house," Papa said.

"If not us, think of your little girls. Maya and Leela are at an impressionable age." Amma advanced her argument. "We will be right next to the road, and anybody could jump over that excuse of a wall. And this area is deserted after dark, except for the drunks and loiterers. After dinner, when you are gone on rounds to monitor students' study hour, I will be alone here with Maya and Leela. Even if I shouted for help, nobody would hear me."

Amma liked our old house in the crowded part of town where she had friendly neighbors living close by. And her place of work was only a short walking distance away.

"What's wrong with the house? It is a huge house with twice the garden you had before," Papa told Amma. "And it is perfectly safe. So don't go about putting such ideas in Maya's head. You know that child will pick up on your fears. And Leela is just a baby. She will love playing outside. Just feel the fresh, cool air." To prove his point, Papa breathed deep and long.

Having registered her protest, Amma gave in to the inevitable. Papa started his new job as a chemistry teacher and athletics coach. Amma rode her bicycle to her job in the town, and I, at six years of age, was enrolled in Mrs. Roy's Montessori School.

Located within a thirty-acre boarding school estate in the small town of Dehra Dun, of what used to be the home of the Forest Research Institute of India, our bungalow-style house was situated right along the campus boundary. It had a long and narrow frontage, bordering Cantonment Road, which led to the nearby old British military camp (now housing the Gurkha regiment) on one end to the town center far away on the other. It was a functioning military area with barracks where liquor could be bought at discounted prices.

Only a three-foot-high wall separated the edge of our property from the road, and we could hear slushy drunks at night as they wound their way to their living quarters along the way. My sister and I would giggle at their tuneless but happy singing and look out through our window with inside lights turned off, so we could see outside without being seen ourselves. Every now and then, a poor sot would pass out right there on the other side of the wall, in the gutter that carried away rainwater to the town drain.

Papa said, "Don't worry. They are harmless, too inebriated to climb even the low wall."

And it turned out he was right on that score. That said, Papa did get a dog to be a watchman, a big, burly, shaggy Alsatian that looked as fearsome as it was gentle.

Then one night, having caught us watching the road one too many times, staying up past our bedtime, instead of admonishing us, he did something that no one had thought to do before. He reversed the orientation of the house. The way it was designed, the front of the house faced Cantonment Road so all comings and goings of our household were clearly visible to passersby.

"This way we have more privacy. They can't see us leaving or entering the house," he said, justifying the move.

The front gate became the back gate, the master bedroom became the living room, the front verandah became the back verandah, and so on. At first, the new configuration created flow issues. Visitors would go to the back bedrooms while vendors like the milkman would walk into the living room. We would laugh about the confusion and walk people around the house so they would get over their embarrassment, and soon everyone got used to it and even came to say it was a better arrangement.

There was another problem with the house. What to do about those twelve tall jamun trees that lined the boundary wall and cast vast amounts of shade? Jamun is a purple, semi-sweet berry, but these trees were too tall for fruit harvest. My father hated cutting healthy trees, so he decided they gave the house character, and he planted pink, white, and purple hydrangeas in a two hundred-foot border underneath all that cool dampness where even grass would not grow.

Hydrangeas love shade, and they thrived. When in full bloom, they were a pleasing, colorful sight. We played games all around them, and later Papa got other more obscure shade plants. And in a few years, our house became a garden showcase, known in all of Dehra Dun. Later bees would make hives high up in the branches so we could barely hear their buzzing, and instead of driving them away, Papa would harvest honey from them, and our house became famous for purple-golden honey that we bottled at home and distributed all over town.

Every time a new master was hired, we had a choice to move, but we unanimously voted to stay. My father would tell the school administration "maybe next time," citing the inconvenience involved in moving. By now, his plants were too precious for someone else to look after.

There was another compelling reason, his garage. After having waited for an eight-year registration period, he had bought a black Fiat for my mother so she would no longer need to ride a bike to work. She would drive. He taught her. In those days, I don't think there was another woman in all of Dehra Dun who drove herself to work. Women were generally chauffeured. He was so proud of her and his shiny black Fiat that he had designed and built with his own hands one completely covered carport on the property. We were the first and, for a while, the only family on campus with a car. So clearly now, he argued with the authorities that he could not move.

"Where would the Fiat stay?"

Bungalows of colonial vintage were not designed with cars in mind.

There was always a good reason to not move, and while other families moved around, I grew up in one house, the residence on Cantonment Road, with a showcase garden, purple-gold honey, and a unique structure we called a garage, a house where I made exquisite memories.

Today a twelve-foot wall exists all along the campus perimeter, and the trees have been thinned on the property. From a security point of view, the house is considered desirable.

But I am glad I grew up in simpler times when, because of having to live in an undesirable house, Papa taught me to face my fears, make the most of what we had, and live life with laughter.

4

COLOR ME HAPPY

I am happy and content because I think I am.

—Alain-Rene Lesage, *Histoire De
Gil Blas de Santillane (1715–1735)*

Today I ran all the way home from school. My mother and I
are going shopping for paint for my room in our new house in
San Francisco. I fidget about in excitement when I get in the
car, but she is cool as she belts me in. She knows exactly what
we need to do.

I hold my mother's index finger tightly, and we walk into
the store.

"Jeena wants to select a color," Mama says to the
storekeeper.

I nod in agreement and smile at him. She chats for a short time with the man behind the desk and then leads me to a wall. It is decorated with colors painted on small squares. Like a rainbow, every color is there. Beneath every square is a name.

My mother bends down on her knees, and we read together. "Ivory. Burnt sienna."

There are so many choices that I can't decide. We are going to get a color that suits us both because my mother loves me and I love her.

"What do you think? How about that one?"

"What is it? P-p-pist-a-a-chh..." I try sounding out the word.

"Pistachio cream." She reads it aloud for me.

"And that one?" I point.

"Tangerine whip," she says.

Pistachio cream. Tangerine whip. What kind of names are these? I think. *Not green. Not orange. But pistachio cream. Tangerine whip!*

My first-grade teacher, Mrs. Allison, has never mentioned colors in this way. In fact, we are learning about the rainbow, and I know the seven colors, ROY G BIV, by heart. Mrs. Allison says I am a good student and smart because I raised my hand in class the other day. I explained how a rainbow was made, that is, sunlight reflecting through those tiny droplets of water hidden in the sky.

Actually I am not so smart. What a cool trick Mrs. Allison has taught us! That helps me remember the order of the colors in the rainbow.

But pistachio cream? I think. *Where is that in ROY G BIV?*

Pistachio ice cream is what I love best when I come home after school for an afternoon snack. Tangerines are my favorite because I love the smell of citrus oil that squirts on the palm of my hand when I push my thumb through the skin on the top to open the fruit. My mother gives me treats after I do my homework, and I usually do that after I come home from school in the afternoon, before I go out to play at my friend Anna's house.

"That one," I say. I know she likes it too.

My mother talks to the man behind the desk. They are busy figuring out how much paint we need to buy. I squeeze her hand to let her know I am still there. And I realize this is it. We are happy as we shop, and tangerine whip is the color of happiness like ours. Pistachio cream is the color of love like ours, and that's why these colors are not just green and orange but also ice cream.

She bends down and hugs me. "Happy birthday, Jeena. I love you, sweetheart."

5

MAYA'S MANTRA

Maya faced the mirror one last time and spread the *dupatta* style long scarf so it draped over her shoulders to display its red and magenta hues. Satisfied with the choice of her outfit, thinking it was chic but not brash, she reached for her handbag.

"I'm leaving now," she informed her roommate. "I have my keys. You can lock up if you go out."

"Is something wrong, Maya? You look sad," Rima said. She sat cross-legged on the bed, still in her pajamas, and looked annoyingly critical.

"You know that nothing is wrong. I am not sad. That's just how I look," Maya said.

"Well, sad is a most unbecoming look when nothing is wrong. And anyway, you know what they say: the last thing you put on is a smile. Look in the mirror, and smile."

"I'm finished dressing, and you are making me late."

"Well then, smile! You are a different person when you smile."

Rima said this all the time: when walking together to class, to the mess hall, to movies, and, without fail, to the University Coffee House frequented by her many fans. Maya didn't care for any of the boys who hung out with Rima.

Usually Maya discounted her roommate's advice. But today was different.

"Okay. Just once. Promise you won't nag me anymore?"

Maya looked at the mirror and scrunched her nose in an imagined laugh. *No. False!* She widened her lips and showed upper teeth. *Better? No. It's a scowl.* She creased her eyebrows. *No. It's an angry look.*

Maya relaxed facial muscles that refused to smile. *Perhaps it is a slight downturn in the upper lip,* she thought. *I'm not a party girl.*

"My look is serious, not sad. What's wrong with serious? It's not like I'm going to a party."

"Serious is worse than sad. It's boring." Rima smiled to take the edge off her advice.

They had applied together for graduate school in America, and in the fall, Rima was joining a college in New York. Maya's application required an interview at the US embassy in New Delhi.

"Your application is already approved. Now they want to check if you will get along in America. You can't afford to look sad, serious, or shy. Smile!"

Maya could not remember the interviewer's name, but later she found it in the letter of introduction she had already put in her handbag. She remembered that he was a University of

Michigan alum. Michigan was where she had secured admission with free tuition plus assistantship for room and board, but with one last hurdle, Mr. Alum's approval.

It annoyed her that the Michigan application required this extra step. Besides the inconvenience, she would have to spend on transportation. She had a tuition waiver from another American university, but Michigan offered financial aid as well. Without it, she could not afford to go.

Maya dreamed of going to America. As much as her vision was about higher education, it also implied escape from upcoming marriage talk. Maya would finish her master's degree in the summer, and upon graduation, when she vacated the dormitory to go home and live with her parents, her wheat complexion would be a topic of conversation, if not downright commiseration, for old-fashioned relatives and neighbors. They would forget that not even the boys from her hometown had gone to America, let alone on a scholarship.

I must ace the interview, she thought.

Not that Maya was unfamiliar with being interviewed, but typically she knew what to expect. Good interviewers involved aged faculty or otherwise renowned notables who grilled her on scientific principles. The bad ones involved old curmudgeons. "Why would women want to study science when they were destined to be housewives?"

It bothered her that the letter introducing Mr. Michigan Alum said nothing of his accomplishments or age. *What if he were a cantankerous type? What qualifications did he have to be interviewing me? Perhaps he has none!*

Maya rallied herself enough to try a smile again. She had no presentiment that the next few moments that she was about to spend in front of the mirror would change her life.

"Experiment. Observe." She resorted to lab drill. "Perturb the status quo. Analyze. Repeat." Maya closed her eyes. She was playing with her pet, a beautiful golden retriever. He reminded her of Aruf, her first dog. How she had loved him!

She opened her eyes. *Better. Much better.*

Last try, a shaggy dog was interviewing her. He woofed. She laughed. She opened her eyes. A lovely, animated, mischievous girl looked back. *Shaggy dog. That's the mantra. Done!*

Maya swung her handbag over her shoulder, straightened her knee length dress style *kurta*, and reminded herself to hurry since the campus was one end of Delhi and the US embassy in Chanakyapuri was on the other.

"Please, God," she prayed. "Make him look like a shaggy dog."

"You look beautiful, Maya," Rima called out from behind her.

■ ■ ■

Jerald was in the second year of a diplomatic assignment in New Delhi after graduating in international studies from Ann Arbor, Michigan. A few weeks back, he had received a call from his friend Milo, now an assistant professor at their alma mater. They kept in touch despite the distance.

"Do me a favor, would you? We accepted a woman from Delhi University. Her grades as well as recommendations are unbelievable. I want you to meet her and confirm that all is on the up-and-up. Talk to her and then call me back. Okay?" Milo requested.

Jerald had objected, saying, "Physics is not my forte. I am a diplomat."

"Interviewing foreign applicants is routine procedure, but sometimes it is not possible. I am lucky you are right where I need you to be." Milo persisted.

Jerald had allowed himself to be persuaded.

"Oh, by the way, set up a Saturday meeting. She has classes during the week."

Truth be told, Jerald was bored with his routine of interviewing visa applicants during the day and evening gatherings with boozy old-school diplomats of dubious distinction.

"What do you want me to do? Poke her to see if she vaporizes?"

"Get your mind out of the gutter. She is only twenty-two years old, probably never dated anyone." Milo had hung up, cutting off further discussion.

■ ■ ■

Jerald didn't mind coming to the office on his day off. The embassy was closed on weekends. It was a relief with no lines of potential visitors or immigrants snaking outside and no chaotic hustle inside. He let himself into the empty building and ran up two steps at a time to his second-floor office. He maneuvered around the ornate, large, and imposing desk which was designed to intimidate and thus elicit truth from nervous applicants, that occupied most of his office. He thought such pretension unnecessary, but he had no say in the matter and the view couldn't be better. Vibrant orange-red Acacia blossoms and light green feathery leaves swayed in the cool December breeze right outside the window. Delhi in the winter months was delightful.

A soft knock broke his reverie.

"Come in," Jerald said.

■ ■ ■

Maya gripped her bag to stop its swaying and strode in. The office was larger than she had expected, as was the man uncoiling himself from the chair behind an ocean of desk.

"Jerald Mann," he said, holding his hand out. "Jerald with a J and Mann with two Ns."

Out of habit, Maya had lifted her palms and brought them together for a namaste. Midstride, she dropped one arm and reached across the desk with the other to shake his hand.

He's American, she reminded herself. Not that there could be any doubt, he was by far the tallest person she had seen with blond hair and a slightly chunky girth that athletes got when they left college to sit behind a desk. *Isn't Michigan a football school?*

"I am Maya Tripathi. I am here for the interview."

Maya was tall for an Indian; nevertheless she felt dwarfed. She didn't like that she had to lean forward to reach his hand and the power dynamic created by the gesture. She wished she had kept her hands folded in namaste. She drew strength from the comfort of her palms touching and the formal dignity of the greeting. *I am Indian, not American.*

Despite the time and money invested, Maya now wanted this visit over. "I thought I was expected. Here is the interview notification from your office."

"Please don't call it an interview." Jerald saw her hands reach for the handbag and realized his informal, relaxed attitude was too foreign and had made her uncomfortable. *This damn desk*, he thought and walked around to stand by her side.

"I am here to ask if you have what you need to join in fall term." Jerald made that up on the spot and smiled, hoping he had reassured her.

Maya had imagined an aged, self-important man questioning her credentials and her right to avail scarce university funds.

As if she hadn't heard a word, she pressed on with the agenda at hand. "I have brought supporting documents for my application: TOEFL scores, GRE scores, recommendation letters..." Maya spoke quickly. She knew about the famous American drawl and had practiced speaking slowly, now forgotten.

Maya pulled out letters, files, handkerchief, and hairclips. She slowed momentarily to look up at him and then continued rummaging to avoid conversation. *Even if it looks fussy, uncoordinated is better than tongue-tied.*

Jerald moved forward, closer to her, and stilled her hands. "It's okay. I don't need to see those. I am only supposed to make sure you are real. You see, your recommendations and grades are so strong that the admissions committee wondered if you might be fake."

Maya saw big hands touching her wrist and golden hairs shining against a tanned-white arm, encased in a starched cuffed sleeve, and her eyes traveled up past his elbows, chest, chin, and blue eyes to rest on a forehead partially hidden by a mop of golden-brown hair.

"It's a routine procedure to interview applicants who apply to Michigan, and I happen to be here in Delhi. That's the only reason I got this job. But now I'm glad I did."

Maya was surprised by how young Jerald was. Commenting on his age would be the wrong thing to say, so she said nothing. Jerald worried that, while interviews by alums might be routine in America, it was not common practice in India. *Was it rude to impose an American custom on a foreign applicant without explanation?* He shook his head, tossing the hair out of his eyes.

Shaggy dog! That toss of the head was adorable. Maya controlled herself. Bag, papers, and *dupatta* were all forgotten. Laughter bubbled up from the pit of her stomach and landed on her lips.

"So am I? Am I real? What is the verdict?" Maya arched up her neck so he could see her full face with eyes wide open and arms spread. She pirouetted.

Jerald saw a shapely nose, high cheekbones, a full upper lip, arched eyebrows, chocolate brown eyes, and a square chin. Prairie gold wheat glowed on her skin. The sudden transformation enchanted him.

"Yes," said Jerald, adopting a thoughtful stance. If he had a beard, he would have stroked it. As it was, he stroked a chin. "I have decided you are real, and I will so inform the admissions committee." He wondered how he could have missed seeing this mischievous innocent when she had walked into his office. "I believe my part of the interview is concluded."

"Why, thank you, Mr. Mann. In addition to references and my application, here are three phone numbers of people you can call who will vouch for me. They will tell you what a hardworking scholar I am and how any institution I select would be lucky to have me."

Is she flirting with me? Or now am I the one being interviewed? Jerald took the papers from her hand and filed them away in one corner of the table.

"Now it is your turn to ask the questions. That is the part I am looking forward to." Jerald picked up his keys and gave the office a once-over to make sure everything was in place. "Would you like some coffee? The cafeteria here is closed today, but I know a great place around the corner that serves authentic South Indian filter coffee. We can talk there."

"Are we done with the interview?" Maya liked closure and was not to be distracted.

"I will call them on Monday and congratulate them on their excellent selection," said Jerald and led Maya out of his office. "I have heard that the coffee house on Delhi University campus has great coffee." He chattered on, fearing, if allowed a word in edgewise, she might say no to the coffee now that the formal part was done. "Tell me how this one compares. I've wanted to visit the campus, but so far there has been no good reason. Besides coffee, I hear it is also the place for stimulating conversation."

Maya had never had coffee alone with a man before. She knew what it could lead to. At the university, she always went out in a group. She didn't want anyone to get the wrong impression.

But she liked Jerald, and knowing full well what it might lead to, she smiled and said, "Yes, I would like a coffee…on one condition though. May I tell you about my best friend? It's my dog. He is shaggy, big, and frisky, yet friendly. And I can't bear to leave him to go to America. Can you help me with that?"

■ ■ ■

Maya joined Michigan in fall of 1970. Jerald finished his term in New Delhi and was posted to Washington, DC. They married and had a daughter. They named her Jeena Maya Mann. Jeena means "life" in Hindi.

Jerald chose the name because he found love and life in the contradiction that was Maya. Maya said Jeena was an unconventional name but approved. When asked why, she said mysteriously that Jeena was like Jerald. She would be having to explain herself to everyone in India as well as America.

6

MY DAD AND THE DUCHESS

A moment's insight is sometimes worth a life's experience.

—Oliver Wendell Holmes Sr., "Iris, Her
Book," *The Professor at the Breakfast Table*, 1860

A literature enthusiast, my dad was into the likes of English poets, for instance, Robert Browning. Other than Shakespeare, since our curriculum in school consisted entirely of American authors I had not come across them. So one day when I complained about the drudgery of school, about the mindless girls who taunted, "She will wear anything as long as it doesn't match," and the bullying boys in the playground, he sat me down and put a book of verse in my lap.

"Jeena, read this," he said, jabbing one long finger on a page that he opened in his book.

He made me read a poem called "My Last Duchess." It was about this duke who, while apparently praising the beauty of his wife, the aforementioned duchess, reveals that he had her beheaded, killed one way or another, because she was just too nice. I didn't get it at first.

I read the poem and asked Dad what his point was. "I don't get it. What does this have to do with my problem?"

And so he took the book from me and read aloud.

> *Her wits to yours, forsooth, and made excuse—*
> *E'en then would be some stooping; and I choose*
> *Never to stoop. Oh, sir, she smiled, no doubt,*
> *Whene'er I passed her; but who passed without*
> *Much the same smile? This grew; I gave commands;*
> *Then all smiles stopped together. There she stands*
> *As if alive. Will't please you rise?*

Dad said the line "and I choose never to stoop" was for the antediluvian and not a modernist like me. He said that complaining in general and especially when others behaved badly would lead me to behave badly too.

"It is an excuse," he said, "to make yourself feel above others. At best, it is a boring habit. You don't want to be boring, do you, Jeena?"

I decided I would be obtuse. "But I am not killing anybody, though they may deserve it. And I am not boring."

"Complaining is boring. Unlike the duke, choose to stoop," he said, "because it means having a conversation."

He said school was more than curriculum taught in the classroom. He said we were all individuals, that is, diverse. And that was why he did not believe in homeschooling.

"School is also learning about people who are different from you. In the playground tomorrow, look for someone, a person you may think you don't like. Say hi and see what happens."

"And why would I do that?" I asked.

"Because you like to learn from books. And learning also comes from people who are different from you."

After I finished yukking, he said, "You don't want to grow up to be like that duke, do you? He missed out on the best things in life because he only knew and admired people like himself."

I finally saw the humor in the macabre situation, though I still told him, "I'm not done complaining."

And he said, "Fine, as long as it's just talk."

And we made a pact.

He and his poems were a strange way to teach a child that others eventually see you for who you are. Deception was not a long-lasting strategy. Those were his words, not mine. So be good first if you want others to be good to you. It was strange indeed. Hence, it was never forgotten.

My dad, long gone now, still brings a smile to my face.

7

UPTOWN GIRL

"Sophistication" is another word for that inventive mix of tolerance, resilience and resourcefulness city people develop.

—Edward Hoagland, "A Year as It Turns," *The Tugman's Passage*, 1982

In a few long strides, the elegant woman clicked her black heels across an expanse of opulent granite to park herself and her wheeled luggage at the lobby registration. She rested a handbag on the polished mahogany, poised to take out a wallet, and smiled at the man behind the counter.

"You have a reservation for me? Jeena Mann. Jeena with a J. And Mann with two Ns."

At forty, Jeena looked thirty and radiated uptown chic. She dressed in Alfani suits, silk shirts, and classic pearls. A

colorful scarf lent flair and drew attention, but with sophistication to blend in upscale surroundings. Even so, this uptown
Jeena diligently nurtured a downtown edge. It alerted her to
danger so she channeled stress responses into positive energy,
and over time, it became her secret weapon in a mostly male
professional environment.

As desired, Jeena's brisk yet warm demeanor elicited
prompt, courteous service. The clerk logged her name into a
computer and then looked up at her. "Yes, Ms. Mann. Welcome
back. I see that we have upgraded you to the executive suite on
the top floor. Thank you for your loyalty to the Mayfair." He
handed her a key card. "If you need something, please allow us
to assist. We wish you a pleasant stay in London."

"Thank you, Ian," Jeena said, noting the lapel badge.
"Yes. Perhaps the concierge can check on theater tickets for
me. Tonight is best, but tomorrow works as well. Comedy or
drama is fine. No musicals, please."

Jeena walked to the elevator and allowed herself a long
sigh. *Finally. What a day!* She was glad it was over. She was in
London for her company's global planning summit, represent-
ing US interests. It was supposed to be a routine meeting, but
it turned out to be anything but routine. No doubt about it,
today had been a disaster. First, her request for an increased
budget was tabled. But that was not the worst part. Despite a
flawless presentation, insubstantial objections from the new
director, Asian Bureau, gained support as the day advanced.
And then solidifying his advantage, he singled her out, the
only woman executive, by insinuating her looks had secured
her a seat in the boardroom.

Jeena's no-nonsense, approachable leadership drew respect and loyalty from peers as well as superiors. Besides impeccable qualifications, Jeena had a reputation for compassion when working with individuals of diverse circumstances, her distinguishing attribute, and she was known for maintaining calm under pressure.

When asked about her secret weapon, Jeena would laugh and say, "Oh, I trust everyone till they give me a reason not to. And they rarely let me down."

While not unusual earlier in her career, it had been a couple years since Jeena last faced a boardroom bully. A rejoinder would sound defensive, so she stayed silent. However, his barbs could not be ignored. Jeena had worked hard to succeed in a man's world, and if left unrefuted, his insult would become watercooler gossip. Perception, not truth, lingered in people's minds.

What could she do? He had said nothing specific. In retrospect, she realized she had missed cues about shifting power dynamics in the board.

Maybe I'm tired after the bumpy flight from California. No, she was accustomed to that. There was another reason. *Am I losing my edge?*

■ ■ ■

Since the concierge had delivered no interesting list of plays, Jeena stayed in. She ordered room service, turned on the TV, and leafed through the in-house magazine. Still she could not relax. Her mind kept rehashing the events of the day without providing any insights.

It was midnight now. Unable to sleep, Jeena padded to the window and looked outside. The area was devoid of walkers. Only a few cars or an occasional bus rumbled along the main road. Several floors below, the Mayfair front entrance lit the area. A smartly dressed doorman stood with authority, a security barrier for loiterers but in place to welcome legitimate hotel guests. The scene before her was typical upscale London Mayfair neighborhood, solitary and peaceful with no foreboding of danger.

I need to go for a walk. Sure, it was midnight; however, the area was as safe as it gets. This was London, not New York or Chicago. Excited by the challenge, Jeena's mind switched course. In contrast to the earlier exhaustion that had enveloped her, a new energy flowed in.

Without hesitation, Jeena went to the closet and rummaged under the work clothes in her suitcase. She did not find her frayed jeans and the faded black T-shirt she used to pack for just such excursions. *It has been several years since I did this.*

Undeterred, she decided travel pants would do. She made the final critical preparations. Then she shrugged on her leather jacket, slipped into walking shoes, and draped a black-and-white plaid scarf, hoping it created a casual look. Effortlessly, she had fallen into an old routine.

As she walked past the night manager, Jeena waved, making sure he saw her.

"Good night, Ms. Mann." If he noticed a change, his training forbade comment.

Jeena stepped out onto the sidewalk that ran along the boulevard, looked around, turned left, and then started walking.

"May I call a cab for you?" asked the doorman.

"No thanks. I want to walk." Gradually, a meditative calm replaced the nervous energy that trickled away from clenched fists hidden in jacket pockets.

The amber glow of streetlights cut through the fog, and she picked up her pace. Each step gave greater assurance. She ventured off the main road, heading into a back alley with occasional lampposts and unlit doorways. Her eyes adjusted to the dark. She sidestepped an upturned trash can and passed by a drunk without breaking stride. A familiar rhythm returned as she noted details and markers. She identified doorways and counted intersections.

Even as a girl, she had an aptitude for numbers and visual perspicuity. With practice, she had developed her distinct safety stratagem, an accurate map of the maze in her mind, so if stalked or otherwise endangered, she could double back or duck into a doorway. Even when she knew an area, she retraced her steps rather than trying a new route. A memory game, the walk helped hone her observation skills, which in turn built confidence in negotiating unfamiliar terrain with a cool head.

After twenty minutes, it was time to return to the hotel. Pleasantly tired, she counted off the intersections, noted the markers, and was satisfied to find she had remembered. *Almost there.*

She turned the corner from the side street onto the main walkway. Maybe it was the sharp turn needed to exit the back alley, perhaps it was the fog, or probably she relaxed now that she was almost at the Mayfair, but she took the corner hurriedly and bumped into a man leaning against the building wall.

"Excuse me," she said as she sidestepped, trying to regain her balance.

"What's your hurry, luv?" He stood, blocking her path. He accented a threatening stance with a salacious smirk.

She saw a muscular man of medium height and build, dressed in a tweed jacket. His brown slacks had seen better days. When push came to shove, he was stronger and a confrontation best avoided. She looked past his shoulder. The Mayfair entrance was too distant for the doorman to see her or help if she screamed. She was on her own.

"Excuse me," Jeena repeated, keeping hands fisted to control their shaking.

"Hey, can you spare some cash? I need train fare to go home. To Scotland." He sized her body and leered. "You know how it is. Spent my money at the pub, and now you come along as my guardian angel." He stood square, arms akimbo, blocking escape.

Jeena unzipped the outer pocket of her small purse. "Here. Take it. This is all I have," she said, giving him a five-pound note and flipping her purse upside down to show it was empty. This was part of the plan. She carried money where it was easy to access.

"It's not enough." He leaned over, swiftly seized the purse, opened the inside zipper, and held out a ten-pound note with a flourish. "I knew it, a toff like you."

This too was on plan. He would expect her to hide something.

"Hey! That's my emergency cash. You can't take that." Some resistance was in order.

He was close now. His crooked teeth were stained a dreadful tobacco brown, and she smelled alcohol on his breath. Jeena backed up two steps, unfastened the purse from her waist, and held it at arm's length.

"Here. See for yourself," she said.

"Give us a kiss then."

Usually after she gave an empty purse, she would be left alone. Then she realized that backing up signaled fear. Now he felt power over her. He pushed her body against the wall, and his arms pinned her to the cold stone. It became impossible for her to move.

"No kiss," she said, putting both palms, fingers splayed, on his chest. She heaved, but to no avail. He moved one arm down to her back and began groping around her hips.

With senses on alert, she realized what he was doing and almost smiled with relief. Out of habit, she had packed away credit cards, driver's license, passport, and extra currency before setting out for the walk. *Good going, girl!*

She let him grope. He would find nothing in her hip pockets, and she wore no money belt under her shirt. She never used a money belt, believing it to be trouble because of the need to disrobe to access it. Plus, it screamed *tourist* and showed a lack of trust in the local populace or, worse, *victim*, which often exploded into adversarial action from an aggressor.

Undecided about his next move, the man dropped his arms, giving Jeena the opportunity she needed. Swiftly, she coiled her muscles to brace against the wall and then pushed hard. He stepped back to regain balance, giving her room to get away from him and onto the middle of the sidewalk.

"I don't want," she said, "to give you a kiss, hug you, or give any more money. I have been good to you. Now it is your turn. You have enough for bus fare. Go home now." She willed herself to stay put and stared him down.

Perhaps it was her confident voice, the shift in power when she was the one telling him what to do, or his interpretation of her words for concern—someone who wants to get a drunk safely home—but suddenly he turned around and shuffled away.

Jeena felt a gust of wind as a bus stopped near her and the door whirred open. She asked the driver without stepping in, "What is the fare to the last stop?"

"Two pounds."

Maybe he was not lying about needing money. A pitiful drunk.

Just then, the man shouted, "I want some love. Bitch." But he continued walking.

After the man disappeared, Jeena walked into the Mayfair lobby.

"Good to see you back."

"Good night," Jeena said.

She keyed into her room, changed into pajamas, got into bed, and called her husband Mark in California. They chatted for a while, and Mark knew her well enough to guess something was wrong.

"All well?" he asked.

"All well," she said.

"How did it go?" he asked.

"Not great so far. I didn't field some curveballs from a new director on the board and was caught off guard. It prompted me to take preparatory action, renewing my edge. The conflict will get resolved now. There are two days of meetings still to go. I am bound to get an opportunity, and when it arises, I will be ready. He will find out that playing victim is not my style."

She did not mention the walk. She never did. *Why worry him?*

8

A CUP OF RESTRAINT

Omar Khayyam wrote, "a loaf of bread, a jug of wine and thou beside me," his portrayal of heaven on earth. To remind myself, I just Googled it, and the first entry that popped up said,

A Book of Verses underneath the Bough,
A Jug of Wine, a Loaf of Bread—and Thou
Beside me singing in the Wilderness—
Oh, Wilderness were Paradise enow!

This may not be an exact translation of the original, but the portrayal is powerful in its simplicity. My teenage mind lapped it up. Even today I can readily recall artists' renderings in my book of poems that I used to pore over—sometimes in color, other times in black and white, but always two beautiful people subscripted with couplets of rhyme.

Yet I, the adult Jeena, in the throes of a breakup with my boyfriend, must ask, "Does Omar's scenario have merit today? In a civilization when we all must rush about so? When we argue, opine, obfuscate, and say the first thing that pops in our mind?"

Short, succinct, and to the point, at first glance, Omar's imagery seemed perfect. No wonder it had caught our collective imagination. There was food for the body and the soul and even a bit of luxury in the form of wine. Or maybe the water used to be undrinkable in those days. Some had also told me that a loaf of bread might be replaced with a leg of lamb for greater authenticity to Omar, but my quibble was not about nourishment. Instead it was about weightier matters.

I imagined Omar lounging under swaying palms, fanned by a gentle breeze, with a bubbling brook beside him in an oasis of pleasure. His beloved came. And then, what if—and bear with me—what if she didn't go along with the idea? What if she—or today it could be he—said, "It's too hot here," "Wine makes me dizzy," "I don't want to sing," "I have laundry to do and hair to wash," or, heaven forbid, "I have to work"? What if it were something along those lines?

Being a man of the times, Omar could say, "Okay then. Bye." And they would part. No harm would be done. But did anybody get what he or she wanted? Where was paradise in this setting?

Now if Omar had added a cup of restraint to his list of necessities, the scenario might have gone differently. From a beloved's perspective, a cup of restraint would mean going with the flow, biting your tongue, lounging around, and accepting the glass. Even half a cup of restraint, in not speaking the first thing that comes to mind, may turn out to be a useful policy.

As for Omar, if his beloved did not want wine or song, let it go. Heaven was still there if the companion were there. Use the other half cup of restraint, and don't push it. I must say I still got the shivers when I remembered Dad's duchess lesson and thought some people need more than a cup, perhaps a jug, flagon, or cask of that restraint.

Be that as it may, the instinct for community was hard-wired in humans. But as we evolved further and further away from the fight-or-flight lifestyle of our ancestors, was the other person in our thoughts, or were we getting too selfish? Community used to be about basics like food and safety. It is different today, but we still need companionship, love, and acceptance. Else, why would we have Facebook? Else, why am I pushing thirty and still single?

And that was where a cup of restraint came in. So I couldn't control my thoughts, but I could control the tongue. Remember a cup of restraint, and give heaven a chance to enter life.

9

UNDERNEATH
THE GUAVA TREE

*I am a hoarder of two things:
documents and trusted friends*

—Muriel Spark, "Introduction,"
Curriculum Vitae, 1992

We grew up together. I was born about twenty-one inches and
seven pounds. He measured about the same. My first memory
of us was one bundle, legs and torsos entwined, rolling around
on the ground. We were inseparable. We were the same height
and weight, and maybe, if it had stayed that way, he would still
be around. He was my best friend and favorite—not to mention only—playmate. I had a name, Maya, and he was name-
less as far as I could tell.

It didn't take long for me to realize that he did everything better than I did. For sure, he didn't need a diaper. He ran long before I took my first step. He could have run away, but he hung around me. I sat and dug stubby fingers into his fur and pulled. He didn't mind. I threw toys, and he fetched. He could jump, roll, and kick a ball. His verbal skills were sharp. He said "woof-woof" while I gurgled "aaaa" or "baaa" and said not a word that anyone could understand. Still, even knowing all that, it never stopped me from bossing him around.

After "mama" and "dada," my next word was "aruf," and that was how he got his name, Aruf.

I should admit, as we got to know each other better, I found Aruf had many qualities I did not admire. He could be positively fastidious, picky, and even snotty. For example, when we would lay flat on our backs, alongside each other on the floor in my room, we measured the same. Later, when he became longer than me, I resorted to stretching my legs and pointing my toes, and my hands stretched way over my head. I would be out of breath, and Aruf would just lay there elegantly, not even making any effort at all. He couldn't be bothered.

When I started walking, I felt justified in grabbing his ear and dragging him outside the house into the garden to sit under the guava tree, a shady, fragrant spot that concealed us, but if I turned my head, I could see grown-ups doing whatever it was they did. On the other hand, he liked the soft, clean carpet in my room and resisted, but I would not give up and he humored me by wagging his tail and loping along. I dug into the soft mud with bare hands, occasionally eating dirt if I thought no one was looking. He would breathe with his tongue hanging out and never tell on me. Sometimes he would dig too, but he never ate mud.

With frequent use, the ground under the tree became muddy, and some roots poked through. I would have to drag Aruf onto the dirt, which was getting harder. To be fair to him, when we played our game, I stretched myself long while he curved his back and pulled in his legs to measure shorter. He would look at me, aslant, as if asking, *Are we done yet?*

He was bigger than I was. There was no getting around it. But I was still boss, and that was okay with him.

At about seventy-five pounds, he was a harmless giant, but his size scared friends who came to play with me. I knew he was being friendly when he sniffed ankles or licked hands. He sported a mutt-bred elegance, an Alsatian face and Labrador body. His tail wagged nonstop. I wished I had a tail too. It was a far better tool for expressing yourself than anything else I knew of. I took to walking around with him in tow. His shaggy yellow-brown hair shone a bright gold in the sun, and with my black hair, we made a pretty contrast.

As the years passed, I got bigger too. Papa said I had to start school. I asked if Aruf could go to school with me, and Papa said no. He did not need to. He said that, even though Aruf and I were both three years old, Aruf in dog years was twenty-one. No wonder he was so smart. I sure needed to catch up.

I was in school until midafternoon so our walks had to stop. Left alone at home with all that time on his paws, Aruf found independence. Papa tried to keep him in the garden, but he found ever newer ways to escape. He found furry friends for company that we knew nothing about. During school hours, he took to roaming the neighborhood streets. Kindly neighbors would escort him back, but he was a free spirit, and he chafed, mewled, and barked when he was tied up.

One day I came back from school, and Aruf was not waiting for me at the gate. I threw a fit. *That no-good bum. How dare he not be at his post!*

But even as I threw my fit, I sensed something was different. Papa held me close, and Mama, who normally ignored my tantrums, hovered around, looking stressed, waiting for me to tire out.

"Why is Uncle here?" I asked, wiping tears.

My uncle lived close by and visited often. He told the best stories. He said he had brought a gift for me. "It's a story," he said, showing me a sheaf of papers. "I wrote it for you. It's called 'Maya's Aruf.'"

I loved his stories, especially ones that started with, "Once upon a time..."

"Once upon a time..." he began.

His story was about a little girl and her dog and how they were the best of friends until one day the dog was no more. Young as I was, I understood. I cried some more but told him to go on and finish the story.

We buried Aruf under the guava tree. Papa himself dug the giant-sized hole so he could stretch out Aruf, who had been hit by a passing truck, mangled but still beautiful in my eyes.

Soon after that, when about four years old, I started reading. Uncle gave me a copy of the magazine with his story, and

I pretty much willed the words into my vocabulary. "Maya's Aruf" is seared in my brain, never to be lost.

Under the guava tree, I read everything I could lay my hands on. On hot summer days, I would sit in its shade and lose myself in a world of words. Words are forever. Friends are forever, especially that part of forever that makes me Maya.

10

BREAD, BOOK, AND CANDLE

You can only lose what you cling to.

—Buddha

When Milo and Kirsten decided on a divorce, their book club friends expected it to go smoothly. After all, both Milo and Kirsten had high-powered professional lives. They were independently wealthy and blessed with good genes in the looks department. Milo was the son of globe-trotting diplomats. Tact flowed in his veins in place of blood. And Kirsten had that old-fashioned hallmark of good breeding, a profound disregard for matters of personal finance.

Money was not going to be an issue. They had no kids. There were no complications on that score either. So the book club never saw it coming, not even Maya.

"Okay, you can have that set of records we bought on our honeymoon" and "Your grandma's armoire is yours, of course. I wouldn't dream of keeping it even though it used to store my clothes." That was how they were.

Material things accumulated over the years did not cause them to bicker or brood. It was to be one of those distinctive California divorces where it was expected that they would remain cordial non-cohabitees. That was how it was supposed to be. That was how it could have been, if not for one thing, their book club.

Later Maya blamed herself and said she should have foreseen the turn that events took. Among the book club members, she had known them the longest. Milo was best man at her wedding with Jerald, and she had met Kirsten in college. When Jerald was killed in a terrorist assault while on diplomatic assignment in Pakistan, Maya suffered from depression, and they looked after Jeena like family.

Relationships were important to them. Maya knew that, and in fact, that was how the idea for a book club had come about. Maya was a founding member too, in a way, because its quirky name—Bread, Book, and Candle—was her input to reflect their personalities. But what could she have done?

The book club discussions were scheduled a year in advance to meet every two months, always at Milo and Kirsten's house. When it came time to meet for a book reading the first time after they decided to divorce, a nascent negativity of discord emerged.

Since their house in Palo Alto was full of memories that would have hampered moving on, they vacated it, put it up for sale, and moved to new separate lodgings. When it was time for the next book club meeting, the question came up. What venue?

Kirsten said, "I will call everyone to my place, okay, sweetie? You must come of course."

Milo said, "Don't bother. We can meet at my place. It's not a problem for me."

The need for a new logistic created the first riff. They had already amicably settled furniture, finances, and photos, but no lawyer had any advice to give on a book club. Unlike an offspring, the state has no opinion on the matter. How do you divide a book club?

"Why would it be a problem for me? My place. I started the club. It's settled." Kirsten was adamant.

"There would be no connections made if I hadn't added the food idea." It was true that Milo proposed dinner with a cuisine to complement the book. He also created the discussion format, developed a website, and kept the schedule updated.

"I will continue with this one. Why don't you start something else?" Milo was web-savvy and a great cook. Kirsten was a reader and lit-savvy.

The book club could only imagine what Kirsten's response was because they were never told.

The first time Milo called the book club together and said Kirsten had to leave town, Maya suspected something amiss. The second time Kirsten had the book club meet at her place, Milo did not attend, and everyone knew.

As Mr Browning has said, "The lark's on the wing; The snail's on the thorn; God's in His heaven…" except "All's *not* right with this world!"

"What's wrong?" Maya asked Kirsten.

"Oh, nothing," she said when it was obvious that there was.

For eleven years, their group of seventeen professionals—couples, partners, or never married; overeducated or blue collar; and sometimes under-romanced—found escape in new fiction as well as classics from Austen to Dickens, Browning to the Bard, and Fitzgerald to Emile Zola. The club had helped them survive an abusive marriage, difficult births, teenage angst offspring, and, in one case, a drug overdose. Over the years, the members had developed an authentic camaraderie, born of passionate arguments over prose, that facilitated sharing not only joys but also secret sorrows.

In Maya's case, it was widowhood. Just like that, without warning, there was a giant hole where her heart used to be. Without her daughter Jeena, there would have been no reason to live. The book club came together to put her back on track. To say that the relationships were merely close would be a profound understatement. Everyone wanted to keep the chemistry intact.

They suggested alternate venues for book readings, but Milo as well as Kristen initially said it would work out. They would alternate houses. It would be fine.

But it was not fine. The group wanted that old feeling of camaraderie to stay unchanged. They couldn't let go. Equally guilty, Milo and Kirsten could not divvy up the subtle pride and achievement they felt in having brought them together. If both happened to be at a reading, they took opposing views, which used to be fine before and even encouraged, with an acridity that begot long, uncomfortable silences.

Soon it got uncomfortable. The food started to taste like shit, and one time when somebody quoted *Little Women*, "blessings become a burden when not shared," about Mrs. March's big house, Sally burst into tears. There were big, big sobs, and somebody had to go get her Evian water.

Roy, the newest member, who had moved to Palo Alto from Las Vegas and ran an upscale eatery on University Avenue, was the first to call and say, "I won't be coming to the discussion any more. The restaurant is getting really busy, and I need to be there in the evenings."

Then one person or another would call Milo or Kirsten and say, "I love you both. I don't want to take sides, but it's difficult to have an open discussion these days. I hope you understand if I stop coming to the club for now. Let's try giving it a break."

Initially both Milo and Kirsten were civilized about it, but later they took to begging. "Please come. It will be fine. Time heals." And so on.

The membership dwindled.

Maya was the last one to call them. "I love you both," she said. "Just remember that."

"Maya, I will start a new book club, and you will be the first one I call," said Milo.

"Maya darling, you are a founder of the book club too. How can you be like that?" said Kirsten

The book club didn't survive the Milo-Kirsten split up. The group could not get together as a book club anymore. Like ghosts, Milo and Kirsten just popped in uninvited, getting everyone all snippy and sad. Yup! There was no more BBC or Bread, Book, and Candle. That was what Maya had named it, a potluck, food-oriented sharing of feelings evoked by a book. They named it that because Maya liked the acronym BBC, having always found the news service good for improving her language skills (Hah!). Milo, the chef, thought that candle signified romance in addition to light, like in A Clean Well-Lighted Place for Books, his go-to bookstore.

Kirsten, the reader, asked, "Who hasn't been chilled by the original phrase of Bell, Book, and Candle with its sinister religious undertones?"

As more people called and said they couldn't come, tensions between Milo and Kirsten grew. Their rancor spilled over into other aspects of divorce until they became vindictive. Previously resolved agreements unraveled. Milo called Kirsten and asked for the records back. Kirsten wanted her armoire back. Now they were even going after one another's trust funds.

They let go of everything they owned that hampered moving on: the house, the furniture, and the money. All except one thing, the book club. They clung to the abstraction that was a group dynamic, and it turned out to be their nemesis. If they had let go, maybe then they would have parted friends.

They could have moved on.

11

NATIONAL HIGHWAY 8 TO DELHI

The question isn't who is going to let me; it's who is going to stop me.

—*Ayn Rand*

Raj jammed the red baseball-cap on his head as he leaned against the hood of his Mahindra Bolero pickup. It might well be a long wait, and the sun was a scorcher. He squinted into the sky before dropping his gaze to stare at her retreating figure. He was in no mood to chase her.

A full two minutes later, she still hadn't looked back. Raj shifted his weight from one leg to the other to ease the pain in his hips, but it didn't work. And he was sweating buckets already. He drummed his fingers on the shiny steel.

Couple more minutes, he thought. *Unless she turns to look, I am riding this baby right home. I'll teach her a lesson.*

She walked straight ahead on the highway. While she was swaying in high heels, the white kurta style dress was hugging her slim waist but swirling below the knees. The tiny yellow sunflowers disappeared in the folds of the skirt and then reappeared with every long stride.

He saw brown hair flowing along her swan neck, glinting as it caught the noon rays. But he couldn't see the welts on her bare shoulders. She was too far away for that.

Raj almost forgot they were there.

She shimmered in the dusty haze, ethereal with an inborn ease, unaware of the sweltering sun. *God, she's beautiful. Sexy too. And unprepared for the heat.* He grinned. *It must be at least forty-five degrees Celsius.*

National Highway 8 from Mumbai, when it passes through the state of Haryana on the way to Delhi, stretches for miles and miles with no shelter on either side, except for the roadside shacks that cater to truckers, and thin electric poles that cast slim shadows in the midday sun. Even the shade of a passing lorry can be a relief. *Not much traffic today. I wonder why*; he thought. *It is midweek. No weekenders to crowd the highway, maybe an odd trucker or random traveler. Nothing to do but wait.*

Raj tilted his cap into the sky for a better shade angle. He couldn't take his eyes off her swaying body. *Should I get in the truck, drive to her, open the door, and ask her to sit? It would be so easy, much easier than roasting on the road… No! This time, dammit, it would be different. She would turn and wave. Then I would drive over to her.*

Raj waited. She kept walking. She was beautiful, yes, but obstinate as a mule. *But didn't I know it?*

Last week, she embarrassed him to no end. She ran away again, and when he fetched her, she complained about the sex. He forced her in bed to stop her grumbling. This time he hadn't held himself in check. The marks showed, so she had to miss her shift the next day. He made up a bullshit story for the dhaba-restaurant owner, saying she was sick, but it wasn't convincing.

Raj recalled the first time he met her. He lived in a one room kholi in the same chawl—tenement style housing—more than a few rows away from her quarters, but the banging and shouting was so loud that it carried clear across the open play area, and the tin-roof shack selling cigarettes and sundries, to his bed. He went to their house to investigate what was going on and found her father ripping into her. He brought her home and told her old man to leave her alone or else.

That was two years ago.

"Could I sleep on your floor?" she asked.

Wanting to help, he said okay, but stipulated that it was for one night only. He supposed she would return home the next day, but in the morning, after one glance at her swollen eye, he let her stay. That was how she moved in. She walked into his life with nothing but the clothes on her back.

Last year on her birthday, all of eighteen, she was a picture of innocence in the white kurta dress with yellow sunflowers she bought from a second-hand clothes shop. She passed twelfth grade with good marks and she wanted to celebrate.

They sat at the bar, holding hands. She ordered a coke, and he had a cold beer. She asked, "Do you know you are my first?"

Then she surprised him by taking two plastic rings out of her handbag, the kind one got for cheap in the local supermarket or roadside stalls.

She handed him one ring and said, "Wear this." Then she whispered under her breath, "I do," as she put the other on her own finger.

Raj, dressed in his work outfit, his only decent one—cap, cotton black-and-red checked shirt, blue jeans, and canvas sneakers—was handsome too. His slicked hair hid the gray, and he forgot how much older he was. He had played along to humor her, slid on the ring, and held up his hand for her to see. She beamed at him with trust-filled eyes, and his chest expanded with self-importance befitting a savior.

The flabby man who was tending the bar had winked. "Found yourself a young one, huh?"

"Keep it to yourself," he'd snapped, but the smirk on the bartender's face affected him, so the novelty of his relationship reduced its luster and somehow changed his perspective.

She didn't care he was twice her age. *Back then, she used to be grateful.*

Raj had helped her get work as a waitress at the nearby Punjabi Dhaba Restaurant and Bar where he stocked inventory and did deliveries. Since his traffic accident a few years ago his back hurt on long drives so he had taken up this gig. It turned out she was a hard worker. She made money in tips too. Customers appreciated her, so now Raj got more prestige, while before the boss scarcely tolerated him with his attitude and frequent no-shows. Also, when he didn't go to work, she made excuses for him, so he kept his job.

He wasn't sure when he disciplined her the first time. Possibly it happened when she tried to move to her own place. She didn't like his drinking and told him he was a mean drunk.

The nerve of her, thinking she could run away. How far can you go, Rima? You need me, or you will faint on the highway.

She waitressed but also applied for other work. He did not see the need. *Hadn't I helped her stand on her feet?* But the Punjabi Dhaba wasn't high class enough for her. She wanted him to get a different job too because nowadays his body hurt after a busy night of hauling heavy goods, and loading-unloading his truck. Also, he didn't get any new long-haul trucking delivery jobs. She said the Dhaba Bar wasn't respectable; it wasn't popular with younger, educated truckers.

Instead of looking for something else to do, he had quit working altogether. Now that she was earning, he much preferred to hang out at the kholi, the small room he rented, and drink cold beer and watch TV. *To hell with her.*

Then one day he had asked, "Why don't you become a dancer at the bar? It's more money, and you can keep the extra."

"Now you want to be my pimp? I won't let you do it—not to me and not to yourself." She stared at him dry-eyed and thoughtful with understanding tumbling into place. Then she got up and walked away.

Sometimes she said, "This roadside slum is no place for me," if he asked what was wrong, but mostly she stopped saying much.

Last night, she was quiet and calm. She hadn't mouthed off in a while, and she grilled chicken. They sat in his room, hanging out. It was nice as it used to be. She had a coke and kept him company.

"I took an evening off," she said.

This morning she said, "Let's go for a ride."

He had agreed, never suspecting what lay ahead. They rolled out of bed and roared down National Highway 8, laughing and getting along fine.

In the truck, she held out her hand and pointed to the ring on her finger. "You know, once you saved me. You are special, Raj." Then she became all highbrow, as she sometimes did. "National Highway 8 is not a road. It is a new start to life. Do you get it? It's the answer to a new me: not scared and not crying. Wouldn't you like that?"

"What's wrong with our life?" Raj had asked. "What I do is drive a truck. As for you, babe, you are a damn decent sight on a dance floor, and this ain't nothing but miles of a dusty, hot highway, hot enough to fry a lizard." He couldn't remember what more he had said.

He wasn't ambitious—food, beer, bed, and her.

It's her own damn fault. Raj was tired of waiting.

Now he remembered what started it. He had said, "There's nothing wrong with bar-dancing. Not everybody gets to be a movie star."

"I don't want to be a movie star," she said. "I want to study and make something of myself."

"Hah! You may be beautiful but you ain't got the brains to go to college." And he had laughed.

"You think so? How do you know? Just because I grew up poor don't make me stupid. Nobody is holding me back, not even you, Raj." Then she had pushed her hand on the horn so it made a headache-sized ruckus. "Stop. Stop. Right. Now."

The pickup was still moving when she opened the door on her side, so Raj slammed the brakes and veered off the road as she jumped out and started walking.

It's a wonder she didn't injure an ankle, twist a knee, or something. Well, she's a natural-born dancer with balance. One hundred and ten pounds of pure muscle, she finished the eight-hour shift without breaking a sweat. How far can she walk before she stumbles or plain passes out? Raj tried willing her into turning. *She doesn't have to walk back. For God's sake, turn your head and look at me. Looks like there's two of her now!*

Raj rubbed his eyes and peered. No, there was only one, but it sure seemed as if she were wading in a cool lake of blue water. She appeared graceful, while here he was with sweat pouring out of his armpits, his forehead, his neck, and just everywhere. *She ain't got the guts to leave.* He'd seen her moods before after one of their arguments. She always returned.

Raj thought he must have nodded off because he almost fell when startled by the noise and gust created by a thundering lorry as it passed. It stopped a short distance away. The dust settled. He saw her hazy form beside it. *She will wave the driver on, and she'll wait for me.*

He saw the lorry raise a cloud of dark fumes and pick up speed as it left the side of the road to get on the highway. Raj narrowed his eyes against the glare of the sun.

The spot where she had stood was empty. No sunflower dress figure stood on the road.

Shit! Raj started his pickup, gunning it into acceleration. *Shit. Shit. Shit.* She did not look, not even once.

Raj maneuvered onto National Highway 8 with wheels spinning, a cloud of dirt in his wake, and foot jammed on the gas pedal. *Good thing it's a highway with nowhere else to go.*

Raj was sweating still, but it wasn't because of the sun anymore. Adrenaline coursed through his veins, heightening his senses. He gripped the steering wheel so tight that his knuckles became bloodless. Then he noticed the ring on his finger. *What did she say about the rings? She would keep hers? What did she mean?*

He thought about her circumstances on the first day he saw her, cowering but defiant in a corner of the makeshift kitchen, when he saved her from her mean old drunk of a father.

Raj shook his head to sort out his feelings. "NH 8 to Delhi is my journey; NH8 to Haryana is yours," he imagined her voice saying. "It's better for you too, Raj."

This time it's about me. She will survive. After all, hadn't it worked out fine last time she walked out of her home with nothing but the clothes on her back?

Raj eased his foot off the gas pedal, U-turned right there on the highway, and headed up National Highway 8 toward his one room kholi.

For the first time in a long time, he relaxed. He glanced at the ring and smiled. He was already planning how he might find her in a couple months, show her the keepsake, and say, "I got it together, babe."

■ ■ ■

Rima joined Delhi University and studied English Literature. At first, she worked as a live-in maid for a professional couple while attending college. Later she secured a scholarship and lived in the dormitory till graduation. For higher studies she joined the Creative Writing Program at NYU in New York, USA.

Her best friend, and college room-mate, was Maya.

■ ■ ■

Raj decided to get treatment for his back problems that did not involve alcohol. He helped at the dhaba as a waiter and later opened his own roadside eatery which offered simple food and clean beds for overnight use to the long-haul truckers that ply National Highway 8. He wanted to thank Rima for saving him from himself, but never tried to contact her again.

He knew what she would say: pay it forward.

12

FEARLESS FEET

May your choices reflect your hopes not your fears.

—Nelson Mandela

As a ten-year-old, I dreaded the unknown—real and imagined. Classes were okay, but the playground evoked agony. I had difficulty making friends. This troubled me, but not as much as it troubled my mother. So in her no-nonsense way, after the school day ended, she enrolled me in one activity after another: soccer, baseball, piano, ballet; you name it.

"Jeena, just try it. You may like it. You'll never know unless you try it," she said.

"I won't go, Ma," I protested.

Mother kept trying until one day when she enrolled me in Theatre Club, I found a passion, and she found a way to give me fearless feet.

I had auditioned for a minor role but got selected to play the lead in our school play. I was the only one who recited not only my lines but other characters' lines as well when they stumbled. We recognized Shakespeare can be a tongue twister. But who knew about my phenomenal memory? Certainly not me, and it became a challenge I wanted to take on.

I needed to go for play practice. But there was a problem. Play practice lasted late into the evenings, after dark, and I would have to traverse many winding lonely lanes to walk back and forth from my house to get there and back home. Besides ghosts and ghouls, who I knew for a fact inhabited the area, what about the occasional kidnapper?

I begged my mother to walk with me. She said she was busy. I laid the guilt trip on her. "Other moms did it!" I said. I knew she would probably be immune. She was. I brought up the safety issue, and she said, "Safety also lives inside you, not only the environment."

"Jeena, you will be safe," she said with enough firmness to throttle further debate.

I played my final card. "Dad would have taken me."

She agreed, but still said no. She was not like other moms. Sometimes I was proud of her, but right now she really bothered me. I thought, *What to do? Do I drop out of the play?*

"Are you afraid of the dark? Moonlight is beautiful," said my mother. "Our neighborhood is safe. I think you can walk by yourself."

"I can't," I said. "I feel someone is going to jump out of the bushes and kidnap me. And then the feeling gets so strong that I run and keep running until I am back home." I decided not to mention ghosts specifically. I would tackle one issue at a time.

"Jeena, it's okay to be afraid. But how does it help to run? If you don't face your fear, it grows and grows, and now, even thinking of it is stopping you from participating in the play."

"But I can't help it. What do I do?" I whined.

"Here's what you do," she said, bending on one knee so she looked me in the eye. "Start by walking at a steady pace. As you get scared, you will find yourself walking faster and faster. Before you break into a run, distract yourself by looking around. You will slow down. When that stops working and you want to run, do the exact opposite: stop dead in your tracks."

"What if I can't?" I interrupted.

"Yes, it will be hard. So after you stop, turn one hundred and eighty degrees so you are facing the back. Plant your feet wide. Stand straight and yell as loud as you can, 'Who's there?'"

"But what if I can't?" By now, I had figured out that my mother would not walk me to practice.

"You can, and you will because I will tell you a secret."

My hyperactive imagination loved secrets, and she had my full attention.

"You have a secret power, Jeena. You have fearless feet. You will discover it next time you go to practice. Your feet are fearless even in the dark, so when your mind takes over and commands your feet to run, you remember this secret, and you let your feet take over while giving your mind something else to do—like yelling or looking around to see if someone is following you. Your feet will not run, and your brain will get time to figure out if there is real danger."

"Got it. Don't run."

"If a dog is chasing, you are better off throwing a stone at it. You can't outrun a dog. If it's a ghost…"

She knows about my ghosts, I thought.

She continued, "Who knows? He or she could be friendly." She smiled. "You can't outrun a ghost either. Try talking to it. And indeed, if someone is chasing you, you can always turn and run again, but your feet will know why, and you will be led by your fearless feet and not by a fearful mind."

One couldn't out argue my mother.

I remembered how she fixed my bed-wetting. While others said I had emotional issues and was to see a psychiatrist, she said there was nothing wrong with me. I just needed to pee. That was all.

At midnight, she shook me awake from a sound sleep, walked me to the bathroom, and put me back in bed after I peed. Next night I woke up when I heard her rustling, and we walked together to the bathroom. Then she watched me from her bed. After that she slept soundly while I went and peed. I haven't wet my bed again. And the nightmares stopped too.

So I should give this new trick of hers a try. *Serve her right if I got kidnapped.*

As if she read my mind, she said, "You are smart. Don't overthink it. Remember your secret, and you will be safe."

That first night, returning after play practice, I found myself shaking even before I started walking. When I was mid way, where the shadows were darkest, the urge to run became stronger than ever. I remembered the secret. When my mind said run, my feet stayed grounded. I fell. I got up, dusted myself, faced the back, and planted my feet wide. In the few seconds it took to do this, my mind shifted from worrying about monsters to worrying, *Oh, I hope no one saw me. I must be looking pretty silly.*

It was like a switch flipped in my brain. That night I learned to be fearless in the dark. Barking dogs and ghostly creatures of the night became friends that walked with me.

"How is the play coming?" Ma asked.

"Great, no thanks to you." In our war of wills, I was not about to acknowledge her contribution. "I am the one walking by myself at night."

"Maya, you let Jeena walk by herself at night?" I imagined my American dad would have said. "How could you?"

"It wasn't easy," I imagined my Indian mother would reply, as if she were the suffering soul, not me. "But it had to be done."

I did not know then about the scent of fear or that I no longer carried it on me.

But I graduated from facing bullies in the playground and small-hearted comrades in college to venturing in foreign lands with people of alien customs and finally to the recessed dark places inside my own mind, like the demons of my ten-year-old self.

Fear is hardwired into the brain, a life-preservation instinct that sharpens the senses and gets the adrenaline flowing, making the body ready for flight or fight. But today, real or imagined, a threat is usually not about life or death, but an opportunity for improvement. I was ten years old when I learned to channel misplaced energy through fearless feet for ghost encounters.

But soon it became a habit that I enlisted into everyday action and thought to create an appropriate response to the situation at hand, to take the calculated risk of facing everything new and different. It may not be danger at all. It might be an opportunity for gaining friendship or knowledge for tapping into inner strength.

As a child of midnight freedom or independent India, my mother knew many women who walked on fearless feet, how they turned enemies into friends, foreigners into neighbors, and barbarians into community. She read about willpower in Indian classics and ancient yoga books. She grew up with values like "unity in diversity" and the sayings of leaders like Mahatma Gandhi. She learned that the only way to break a cycle of cruelty was through compassion.

At ten years of age, I did not understand Gandhiji's exhortation of courage for peaceful action, "If someone slaps you on one cheek, turn your face and show them the other cheek." Today it is a habit in my negotiations, for work as well as personal life. I understand that taking a calculated risk to open a communication channel is an act of courage and the only winning strategy. In civil society, flight or fight is not a long-term win-win approach. Today I treasure mother's grit. She taught me there is nothing to fear, not even fear itself.

Maybe it's the political climate or our enhanced expectation around safety and security, but these days I meet more people who handle unfamiliar situations with a great degree of trepidation, if not downright fear. The adage about what we don't know we fear and what we fear we destroy seems truer today than when I was growing up.

Or Ma's precious secret of fearless feet gives me the courage to look for security, not in my environment but within myself.

13

THE INTRUDER ON OUR BALCONY

Accept that some days you are the
pigeon and some days the statue.

—Dilbert [Scott Adams], http://www.
grinningplanet.com/funny-quotes/
pigeon-quotes-funny.htm

My day started as it usually did, a beautiful sunny morning with a cool breeze in our aerie-nest home in my city of Dilli, or New Delhi, as they called it now. Dilli, "If there be heaven on earth, this is it, this is it," as penned by a Mughal king who, I guess, fancied himself a poet too. Sundari nudged me awake with a gentle tweak of her beak and whispered coo-coo.

I stretched, fluffed my feathers, and thought, *Oh! All is right with the world.* Little did I know.

I tickled Sundari back, making her puff herself in a blush. The city slept or slowly wakened below us in the early light of dawn. We fondled some more before soaring off in perfect symphony into the air, swooping and playing with the breeze. Then we neared our favorite morning perch, the corner balcony of apartment 801 on the eighth floor of Central Park in this new area of Dilli. It was where we rest in the morning before going for breakfast. We had been doing it for so long that others had given up coming there now, and we claimed it as our own special, private family place.

So it came as a shock when I sighted the intruder. "Sundari, look. Someone is perched in our balcony. Do you see him?"

"Yes," she said. Her face was all tight. "He reminds me of that magician's horrible monkey who escaped and used to snarl and snap at us when we flew anywhere near him. He smelled bad too, and he was so dirty. I was so thankful when they caught him and took him away."

"But this one is not moving at all, and he looks much smaller than the monkey."

"I don't care." She sniffed. "Let's fly away."

But I wasn't ready to give up our family nook just yet. We flew closer, and I saw that the intruder sat quietly, still as a rock. I was not wanting to argue with Sundari. I knew how she could get. I swooped down and positioned myself about three yards to his right.

Having no choice, Sundari perched herself on his left, at first far away, but then she edged closer until she was exactly three lengths away too. Then she gave me a dirty look. I cooed at her, hoping to relieve her nervousness. I also wanted to alert the intruder of our presence. Maybe he would go away.

The intruder sat immobile, as if we weren't even there. We stared intently at the stranger. I screeched, fluffed feathers, and swooped up and down, but there was nothing. No response. I inched closer. Sundari moved too. Nothing.

We were there doing so many antics and making so much noise that I soon spotted the flat owner inside, behind the window curtain, looking at us. He called his wife, and she came. I saw that they started laughing. They lived in America and visited the flat in wintertime. The wife's name was Jeena, and the husband was called Mark. They were quite sweet, and unlike other flat owners, they didn't shoo us away.

"Well!" I huffed. "I live here all year, and I am not giving up this place, even though this stranger is no friend."

I saw Mark bring out his camera, but by then, enough was enough, so Sundari and I swooped away.

As you can well imagine, this whole episode quite disturbed Sundari. She couldn't forget the time when the monkey had invaded our space, but she had agreed that this stranger was no monkey. As the sun set over Dilli, we flew back to our home. Far away in the distance, I could see our balcony. I sighed, wondering if tomorrow I would have to go find a new morning perch.

Now it was getting dark. Twilight dusk bathed the landscape. I looked toward our balcony, loath to say good-bye.

Then suddenly, as if he had seen me looking, the stranger glowed a welcoming light as if saying, *Hello. Come join me.* I was dumbstruck. But yes, there he was—winking, blinking, and shining, sending warmth and friendship across the distance. We pigeons could not do this.

How would I signal back?

"Look, Sundari. Look at our balcony. Do you think the stranger is calling us?"

"I don't believe it. Looking so friendly, he is bright and cheerful, not like the monkey at all."

All through the night, he glowed until we started to wonder if he were lonely. We couldn't wait for dawn. We got up earlier than usual. It was still dark outside, and there he was, calling us with his glow. We flew straight to the balcony without any of our morning play and perched on either side of the stranger.

"Sir, would you like to be our friend and share the morning perch with us?" Sundari invited just as the sun rose in the east, flooding the balcony with morning light.

In response, the stranger stopped glowing. Once again, he became still as a rock, as if not wanting to intrude in our ritual but happy to be near us, like a member of our small family.

I heard the flat owner calling his wife from behind the curtain. "Jeena, come here. You know that solar lamp we brought with us for lighting the balcony? Looks like the pigeons have adopted it."

"I am glad. Ma told me that, in the olden days in India, pigeons used to get a lot of respect. In the old city of Dilli, in historical areas like Chandni Chowk, rooftops were the place to be to feed pigeons and fly kites in the evenings. We don't feed them, but if they like the solar lamp, I am happy."

They fussed and took pictures of the three of us—Sundari, myself, and this stranger they called "Solar Lamp"—with a fancy new camera that I noticed. I preened my thanks to the couple for bringing us a new member in our family.

All was right with the world again.

14

ONE EVENING IN THE PARK

How easy 'tis, when Destiny proves kind
With full-spread sails to run before the wind!

—John Dryden, "Astraea, Redux," 1660

An oleander hedge that blooms wildly with red, white, and pink flowers most of the year hides McKenzie Park from the hustle of Foothill Expressway. Cars can access a small parking area adjacent to the park via a narrow tree-lined lane that runs parallel to the expressway, along the hedge. It sees hardly any traffic, and usually the park is quiet and uneventful.

McKenzie Park is where Jeena occasionally brings a lunch sandwich to eat and to get away from office gossip. It is near her work. Fall, when the leaves turn color, is her favorite time of the year. When the maple trees are gold, yellow, and orange, and the park is carpeted with dropped leaves, she stops by in the evenings on her way before going home to rustle her feet in dry, leafy mounds, to smell the moist earth, and to feel the roughness of the bark and the softness of the grass. Jeena likes the park's isolation. She hardly ever meets coworkers there, but she avoids it after dark as a general safety precaution.

That fateful evening, Jeena was late getting out of work. A strategy planning session took longer than scheduled. When Jeena looked at her wristwatch, she realized it was too late to attend her yoga class at the gym. She needed the exercise, and it was early yet to go home to television and dinner. So she thought of going to McKenzie Park. Fall was giving way to winter, and the days were getting shorter. She had not been to the park this late before. *Why not? It's twilight still.*

On impulse, Jeena steered her Prius off the main road to get to the side street accessing the park. The dwindling traffic noise convinced her that she had made the right decision. She rounded the small shopping center with its homey restaurants and grocery store on the northern edge of the park, headed past the few old houses, eased into the T-junction of the parking lot, and almost ran into the dog.

■ ■ ■

The man was lounging in the park with discontent oozing out of every pore when he heard a car door click. He ran to hide behind the bushes and saw a petite woman walking away from her car, toward the open space in the middle, carrying a yoga mat. She was alone. He smiled with satisfaction.

■ ■ ■

Absorbed in her thoughts, Jeena had not seen the big black dog lurking in the corner until she was almost upon him. Wanting to make sure he was unhurt, she stopped roadside and got out. Jeena was good with dogs, and typically they came when she called. But this one kept his distance. It was not a friendly dog and would not come to her. He looked away as if he wanted her to leave. He had no collar, and he tucked his tail between his legs but stood his ground.

She searched the area nearby to see if his identity tag had fallen off but found nothing. The dog watched her closely. Feeling sorry for him, she waved to him as she got back into the Prius, re-parked it properly, and got out. He followed her with his eyes, and this time, he wagged his tail when she waved from a distance. Clearly he was not hurt, and if he was telling her something, she did not comprehend. It now seemed to her that he had come under her car on purpose to make her stop. But then, if he wanted to be friends, why had he not come closer? Was he giving a warning of some sort?

Ten minutes, she thought. *It would not be dark for at least another ten minutes.*

The park was deserted. She walked to the middle open area where the lawn was widest, spread out her mat, and sat down cross-legged, breathing deeply. She had the music on her smartphone but did not bother turning it on. She knew her routine well enough, and she liked the stillness of the park.

One. Two. Three. She felt tension draining away. Her body relaxed. Traffic sounds became louder and, when acknowledged, went away. Now she could visualize her soft breath. Inhale, and exhale. She experienced the breeze whispering in the leaves.

Then suddenly a dry twig crunched, and her eyes flew open. A dirty, red-eyed, mean-faced man had appeared out of nowhere and was looking at her. He blocked the path to her car as he lumbered toward her. There was nowhere for her to run.

Jeena stood up and started rolling her mat, preparing her getaway. What should she do? *Are you supposed to talk in such a case? Or are you supposed to ignore them?* She stared at the man, making eye contact to communicate she was not afraid. Fear had its own smell that incited the aggressor. She noticed he was much bigger than she was with muscled legs and arms.

Out of the corner of her eye, Jeena saw the black dog she had seen earlier near the parking lot. He had followed her, and now he was watching her face, watching the man's back. In that instant, Jeena knew what to do, what the dog had been trying to tell her. She held out her hands, looking at the man directly and past him at the dog too.

"You can have my money," she said to the man to hold his attention, to keep him from turning and looking back.

She need not have worried. The dog moved forward soundlessly.

"Yeah. That too."

In that same moment, when the man lunged at Jeena, knocking her off her feet onto the hard ground, she saw the dog race, leap into the air, and land on the man's back.

Caught by surprise, the big man lost his balance. He had not heard or seen the dog coming. He fell on top of Jeena with the weight of the dog on his back, and sharp teeth sank in his neck.

He hated dogs, and this one snarled like he was not going to let him go. Somehow he untangled himself and got up. "Another day," he said and ran. He was immediately swallowed up by the bushes bordering the park. As if he had never been there, the man was gone.

■ ■ ■

In the scuffle, Jeena picked up some scratches and twisted an ankle, and she felt a lump growing on the back of her head. She called the dog, and this time, he sat on his haunches near her and gave her a wise look. Then he came closer and sniffed her hands, as if making sure she was okay.

"Do you want to come home with me?" She thought he was clearly a stray as she buried her face in his soft neck and finally allowed herself to sob her relief.

Then she heard a whistle followed by a shout, "Max! Max! Where are you, Max?"

Jeena peeked out from behind the black fur, still sitting where she had fallen. *What now? It's not over yet?*

"I am so sorry. Is Max bothering you?"

Jeena looked up at the man towering over her.

"He ran out so suddenly that I could not catch him. He never does that. We come to the park for a walk in the evenings, but he always waits patiently for me. Not today. When I came home from work and let myself in, Max charged out without so much as a hullo!"

He bent lanky legs, and Max went to him, wagging furiously, clearly excited by seeing the newcomer.

"What came over you, Max?" He put on Max's collar and leash combo.

Max looked smug. The man looked relieved to see the dog. *He looks more worried about the dog than me*, thought Jeena.

"He is not bothering me," Jeena said to get his attention.

"Oh, I am Mark, by the way, and this is my dog Max."

"Max saved me from an attacker so perhaps he knew something you didn't, and that's the explanation for his unusual behavior."

"What does that mean? Are you hurt?"

"I am fine now, thanks to Max." Jeena called Max, and he came close enough for her to hug him again.

"I don't believe my eyes. Max doesn't like strangers, yet he seems to have befriended you."

"Why, you sound jealous! I like dogs, and they like me. It's that simple."

Finally she had Mark's full attention. *He has liquid eyes, long lashes, and a gentle touch.* He caressed the scratches on her arms.

"I was so worried about Max that I didn't realize you were hurt. What happened?"

"If you want, we can get a cup of coffee around the corner, and I will tell you how Max saved me."

"Now that sounds like an offer I can't refuse." Mark smiled.

"Then help me get up. I have a twisted ankle and a bump on the back of my head that is causing me not inconsiderable pain. Will they have ice at the coffee shop?"

Mark looked at Jeena's wild hair, oval face, shapely nose, and mischievous eyes that sparkled at him. He felt a sudden urge to move the hair away from her cheek, but he held himself back. "Really? An attacker? You don't look scared or angry." He held out his arm to help her up.

"Whatever occurred was for the best. If it weren't for what happened before, I wouldn't have met you," Jeena said and quickly added, "Or Max."

With Mark's help, Jeena stood up and then rotated her ankle to loosen it, and they started walking. Max ambled along on her side, not Mark's, as if challenging the man who had attacked earlier to try again, if he dared.

"I don't know what spell you cast over him, but Max likes you far too much for my comfort," Mark said, noting Max's unusual behavior. But this time he didn't seem jealous. He sounded as if he approved. As if he liked it, in direct opposition to his statement.

"No spell. No words. We have synergy. I did my part so he could do his. We are a team. That's why he likes me."

"I am his team. He didn't know you until a few minutes ago." Mark pretended to be aggrieved.

"Maybe he knew me in a previous life. Perhaps now we three are a team. Are we, Max?"

Max responded with a wagging tail.

"In a previous life?" Mark couldn't think of anything witty to say so he pretended to not understand.

"Or perchance it's destiny."

"Do you believe in destiny?"

"Ten minutes ago, if you asked me that question, I would have said no. But now I am not sure. Today is the first time I am in McKenzie Park this late, the first time Max ran out on you, and the first time I encountered a vagrant. And then we met. So tell me, what is destiny if not a random juxtaposition of unusual, unforeseen events?"

As they sauntered along, of the three, Max was the calmest and most in control. The other two at some point, even before they reached the coffee shop, were holding hands, and Jeena leant further into Mark's shoulder, as if easing the ankle sprain, but really she was only allowing destiny to do what it will.

15

THE BUG AFFAIR

*A Lady's imagination is very rapid; it jumps from
admiration to love, from love to matrimony in a moment.*

—Jane Austen, *Pride and Prejudice*, 1813

A funny thing happened at the gym today. There I was, sweating on the treadmill and thinking about things, mostly the application I was working on, not getting anywhere. Then it so happened that I looked up, and the TV monitor facing me advised, "Life is too short. Have an affair."

Before I give the wrong idea, let me just up and say that I love being married. In fact, I love it so much this is my second time doing it. *But have an affair?*

The talking head on the monitor cited a random—or possibly psychology—study that gathered enough data to conclude that paying attention to someone at work or elsewhere gets us to dress better, to have more energy, to be more vibrant, and to be on our best behavior. In essence, when we are attracted to someone else close by in addition to a spouse, it makes us more agreeable and productive.

I showered, toweled myself dry, and mulled on this piece of wisdom. It didn't say to have an affair because it was easy to come by, like going in and out a door, which would have been my theory. Easy in, easy out. They said it was good for you. Psychologists, what do they know that I don't?

Good for you? I pondered. Is it about *passion*? Like—be passionate about what you do? But passion is a hammer. Just like a hammer on fruit, passion explodes and shatters lives or just like a hammer driving a nail, passion brings two people together to make a whole new entity: marriage. I am not sure an affair is where passion should lead.

On the drive to work, I rationalized this information with respect to my routine and daily behaviors. I admit to admiring healthy bodies, both men and women. I follow fashion trends, what my coworkers wear on casual Friday as opposed to Monday through Thursday. At a party, I seek out interesting conversation, especially if it comes from a person not in my regular collection of friends. I like to eat at a restaurant I haven't eaten before. When it comes to books, I find my own authors, not best-sellers from the *New York Times*. There is truth to variety being the spice of life. I agree that discovery is energizing. *But an affair?*

And then I got it. It's like me and software bugs. I am passionate about them. One thing I know: somedays I just *love* bugs. In fact, on day five of writing code for the same elusive function and making no headway, when I got bored, I just go and fool around with bugs. Easy come and easy go. No commitment and no hard feelings. And since we worked off a defect list, nobody bothered me because the next release was eons away. Taking time off to fix a bug felt like I was Vegas-bound instead of desk-bound.

Hours flitted by like seconds. On the other hand, seconds seemed like hours when I was stuck writing code that didn't want to emerge from the recesses of my brain. That critic inside me was silent when coding for a bug. What was to criticize? A bug was a bug. And those bugs, the best toys ever, sometimes gave instant gratification, and for variety, occasionally they confounded. Yes, it was true. A programmer knew and needed her bugs.

It didn't help to disparage the design document, curse the architecture, or write mediocre functions that didn't do enough to justify the memory they fragmented. Right there in the middle of the page, when boredom struck, I quit coding. I gave up. That was no slight to my grit. It was just fact. I was practical that way.

As a development engineer in a software company, I was assigned a bug list, and sometimes it was quite the prescription for coder's block. I saw no shame in reaching out.

If that day I fancied myself a minimalist, I took up a lightweight bug. We rated our bugs one to nine, with one being the easiest. Other times, in a burst of extroversion, I attacked a heavy nine. They were usually graphics or user interface bugs, and programmers know there is no right resolution. You could go at it for a while. They were heavy on the photos, logos, and pics, and because my profession was pixels (not pixelated), I felt obligated to expound. Then occasionally I fixed machine code because I found myself introverted too.

A bug offered variety. A software bug spoke to me because I had no idea what I wanted when I was stuck, feeling uninspired. I fixed bugs more often than I liked. It was a guilty pleasure, and I didn't want anyone to know if it were three hours or five days I spent away from my main assignment. Eventually I got bored with fixing bugs, and I went back, rejuvenated, to coding the application I was committed to. In the long term, it was what I loved to do.

But an affair? How easy would it be to go back? I would stick with bugs. Thank you.

16

MARGARITA LOVE

If your life at night is good, you think you have
Everything; but if in that quarter things go wrong,
You will consider your best and truest interests
Most hateful.

—Euripides, *Medea* (431 B.C.), Tr. Rex Warner

Sex is a drink. It feels great, and its anticipation is even better than the first sip, like a cold, cold margarita on a hot summer day. That is how I am with him, exciting flavors of salt, tart, and sweet, all in the first touch. But after too many drinks, what I am left with is a sour mouth and broken glass.

That's how I am when I wake up this morning. It helps me decide and tells me what I must do—what I haven't done before—though this is not the first time it has happened.

He did it again last night.

In my head I craft the sentences for our talk—the conversation—I plan to have with him, as I brush my teeth. I comb my hair and say the words out loud. I practice the punch line, as is my habit for customer presentations at work, even though this time it is personal. I practice till I am satisfied I can do it.

He is in the kitchen making omelets. He whistles his happiness. I clear my throat a few times with great deliberation before walking in on him. The effort makes me nauseous again but I don't want to look weak or tentative so I stand across from him, lean on the granite topped island counter and breathe; shallow, noisy breaths, but they do the job. My voice is steady when I speak.

"I have something to say to you."

"I know what you will say." He grins, turns, and scrunches his lips to drop me an air-kiss. "*Mwah.* I love you too, Gorgeous."

It is our routine. His morning *bon-homie* puts me in a good mood. I wake up grumpy and he wakes up cheery. Usually it makes me weak in the knees from wanting him, but not today. It has no effect on me today.

A headache builds immunity to masculine charisma. Or maybe I have had enough of his lies.

Either way, I stick with the words I practiced in front of the bathroom mirror.

"This is important. Listen. Give me your undivided attention." My voice is even stronger this time. It gives me confidence.

"Shoot. I'm all ears." He is whistling again.

I pull up a stool and sit down.

I realize he has no idea what's coming. *Heck, why would he? Yesterday, even I had no idea it would come to this.* After all, we have been married for two years.

"We can't go on like this."

"Like what?" He leans over, lands a peck on my cheek, and continues whisking eggs.

"Look at all this." I wave my hands at the remnants of last night.

"Looks like we had us a good time, Gorgeous."

He has enough charm to equip a dozen bracelets.

"You don't remember, do you?" I soldier on with the pre-planned dialog, hands twisting a strand of my dark hair; hair that, he says, is his biggest turn on.

"I remember silk skin, musk, a feather touch, and… should I go on? Don't say I didn't warn you!" He laughs and almost has me forgetting myself.

My heart mutinies. I am glad I sat. It's easier to squish a thumping heart when sitting. *Do I really want to do this?*

Fortunately, my head holds firm. It says *do it* even though it is Jell-O from all those margaritas last night.

With shoulders squared, I move out of his reach. "I will shower now, and when I come out, you are to be gone."

"Gone? Gone for the day? You have me for the whole week, Babe."

He is in sales and travels fifty percent of the time but when he is in town, he's all mine. I am a programmer with flexible work hours but my schedule varies depending on what stage my project is in and customer meetings.

"No. Gone for good." I hate myself for bursting his bub-bly humor. I hate him even more for hurting me without even knowing.

"Hey, what did I do? Is it my fault I can't get enough of you?" He closes in, places his arms on my shoulders, bores his guiltless eyes into mine, and smiles.

He is not so innocent I remind myself.

"That is not the problem." I am surprised how firm I sound. It gives me the upper hand. Practice helps.

"What then? What happened? Tell me." He is guileless, another adorable trait. But I have his full attention now.

On the one hand I want to stop myself so I don't hear what he will say next but on the other, I also want to hear him say it. Otherwise my plan doesn't work.

I get on with it and give him the test.

"What is my name? Say my name."

"Jeena. Of course, I know your name."

There it is; the cue I've been working for so I can shoot the final bullet.

"Not last night. You didn't know my name last night. And not other nights after a few drinks. Then you say *Margarita*. And how you say it—wistful, tender, and loving. With *Jeena*, it is rough and tumble, like we are buddies. I had hoped my love would change things. But for you, it's Margarita you love, isn't it?"

"I love you," he says with eyes downcast.

This is the exact evidence I need to feel justified in carry-ing on; finishing what I had started.

"I think, in your own way, you do love me, and last night we had too many margaritas. But for now, it's one too many *Margarita*. I need a break from you."

It's a Mexican standoff: him, me and the invisible Margarita.

We stare at each other till the tea kettle whistles, demanding action.

Then he wipes his hands on the kitchen towel, turns off the fire and reaches behind his back to untie the apron which says *Kiss the Cook*.

I leave him alone to go shower. I turn on the music box in the bathroom with the volume on high, loud enough to drown sobbing noises in case he comes to get his clothes.

Sex—too much and we forget about love.

I have no regrets.

Now he is gone and what I am left with is a bad hangover. But I am also free.

Free to fall in love.

17

MY FIRST FRIEND

*I love you when you bow in your mosque, kneel
in your temple, pray in your church. For you and
I are sons of one religion, and it is the spirit.*

—Kahlil Gibran, English Edition Publishers
and Distributors (India) Pvt. Ltd.

His name is Mahmoud. I don't think anything of it even
though I know no one else by that name. True, my mother's
name is Prakash, and I have another aunt by that name. My
father has a brother-in-law with the same name as his. So does
Uncle Sheel. But then my name is Maya, and I don't know anyone else by that name either.

I would be playing in the front garden and Mahmoud
might come to see my father. He was always dressed in his

crisp uniform: white jacket, white pants, and shirt. And he smelled clean.

"Where is your papa?" he would ask.

Before I could run in to call my father, he would bend over and say, "Here, I brought something for you." And he would open his palm, revealing a lovely piece of candy, savory, or something.

As I got older, he would tell me more about his day, and I would tell him my secrets. Sometimes, if he had time, he would walk me to school. It took only fifteen minutes, but it made me happy enough to last a long time. If I got tired, he would give me a piggyback. Other days, we raced, and I always won.

"Come on, slowpoke. Run faster."

I would laugh and push his back.

Sometime later, Papa told me that I should not take candy from Mahmoud.

He said, "Now you are older."

"But Mahmoud is my friend," I said.

My father would pause and then say, "Well, it is his share of the candy that he saves for you. I guess it is okay if he wants to but know that it is not an extra piece."

Mahmoud worked as a bearer in the mess hall in the boarding school where my father taught, and as part of his job, he had been trained to teach rowdy students proper table manners and to chew with their mouths closed. I knew that his wages were meager, but his food and housing was free.

We spoke Hindi at home, but in school, we had to speak only in English. And when I walked to school with Mahmoud, at his request, we started talking only English. Pretty soon Mahmoud had a better accent and knew more words than I did. After about a year, I noticed Mahmoud would come to our house and speak to my father even in English only.

"I want to be a schoolteacher," he would say.

One day I came home with my clothes all torn.

"What happened?" asked my father.

"I had a fight. When I said my best friend is Mahmoud, the boys said he is my friend only because you give him money. Is this true, Papa?"

My father held me close. "That is not true. Sometimes I lend him money, but he always pays me back. He is saving to get married. He is too proud to take money, but he is paying a tutor, and I want to help him."

I remember the day when Mahmoud came to say good-bye. He was very happy. He got married, and he got a job teaching English to little girls and boys.

My father was happy for him and asked, "Why a good-bye?"

Mahmoud and his new wife were moving to a small village near Lahore, which was now in Pakistan since partition. *Partition* was only a word for me. I didn't know much about it because it happened a few years back, just about the time I was born. And Papa didn't like to talk about it when I was around. All I knew was that Pakistan was not India and he was going far away.

I cried, clung to his waist, and said I would not let him go.

"I'll be back to visit you so soon that you won't even have had time to miss me," Mahmoud said and dried my cheek.

But I never saw him again. If he came to visit his family and his in-laws in India, he did not visit us. I heard from my classmates that my friend, my first friend, the gentlest, most refined, most loving friend, was no longer the person I had known. He was not welcome in India.

"His wife has to wear the burka-type body cover now because that's how it is in that village," they said. "He follows their rules. She never covered herself with a burka in India. Even his in-laws don't think it's right," they said.

And then there was the ultimate letdown. "Who knows if he is able to teach as he wanted?"

I fought with my classmates and shouted that they knew nothing, though something inside me recognized that what they said was possible.

After partition, when India was split into two countries by a line on paper that cut through houses, tiny villages, and populous cities, my uncle Sheel and his family escaped bloodshed by running away. They came to live with us until he found a new job. When we visited him in him in Delhi, he said he missed his old home in Lahore, but he would not go back.

"It's different there now," he said. "My friends have changed too."

And I thought that, in his new home, if Mahmoud had found a first friend like I had, a friend who saw future in the eyes of children, maybe he would have changed his village instead of his village changing him. And then there would be no violence against women and no bloodshed of teachers.

And no change in my memories.

18

A WALK IN THE WETLANDS

Look for a lovely thing and you will find it
It is not far—
It never will be far.

—Sara Teasdale, "Night," *Stars To-night,* 1930

The wetlands behind Shoreline Park, just a short distance from Highway 101 but a whole world apart, are magical today. Finally, after a year of severe drought, we have had a month of hard rain, enough to bring the water level back up to the edge of the walking trail.

Water has been pouring from the skies with the intensity of a monsoon, every drop fat and full. Sometimes it reminded me of July in Delhi when, after months of scorching heat, the heavens opened up to share their bounty. I remember running out fully clothed to feel the raindrops on my face. I would look up, savoring every droplet individually as it hit the inside of my cheeks. It was heaven on earth.

As I walk in these wetlands today, I think, *This must be how the egrets feel, heaven on earth.*

They are out in full force. It is cloudy, cool, and foggy; perfect wetland weather. What looks like steam rises from the water, pure white in sharp contrast to the dark, almost-black outline of the scrub, which hides flora and fauna from the eye. But not the egrets. Everywhere I look, it seems like hundreds of tiny, snowy birds swim around, frolicking gracefully and purposefully, perhaps to celebrate this gift from God and to give thanks or perhaps just be themselves.

As my eye follows one group, I see one bird all by itself. From a distance, it seems small so I walk on the path toward it, convinced there must be other birds around it. Unlike the small egrets in groups, this one is a much bigger bird, also in the heron family but with large white plumes that sheath water off its back. It is a great white egret, regal in bearing, looking away from the rest. It is all by itself. There is nothing else like it all around as far as my eye can see.

Why is it alone? Is it sad? Is it happy? Then I see it is not alone. A perfect reflection gives it company. It does not look lonely, just quiet and reflective. It takes a tiny step forward and then another and another, and the reflection moves along in perfect harmony.

I too take a tiny step toward shoreside and look at my reflection. *What do I see? Is it Maya? Is it Jerald?* I touch the water surface with the tip of my finger, and the reflection comes alive in the ripples that expand and grow large, and I see it is us—both of us—in this heaven that exists on earth.

Nature gives us shadows in the sun, echoes in the mountains, and reflections in pools so nothing need ever be alone and lonely. Memories are but reflections of the soul. Nature gives me memories. I must try to remember only the love we shared and forget the jihadi hatred of Pakistanis who killed him in the name of God, of Allah. Jerald would have forgiven them.

Jerald is as inseparable as my reflection. I need only look, and I will find that he lives within. His love will last me seven lifetimes.

Before I take a picture to etch the scene in my brain, I give thanks to those around me who work to save these wetlands from the encroaching city where I live, where I must bring up my daughter Jeena to be strong. I don't know yet how I will do it. But I know that the answer lives here in these wetlands with Jerald. He will guide me.

19

THE OPEN DOOR

*Are you then unable to recognize a sob
unless it has the same sound as yours?*

—Andre Gide, *Journals*, 1922, Tr. Justin O'Brien

The door is open.

Why is it open? What is in there, past the open door?

Arms folded on my chest, stooping as if to block the world, I march across our front lawn and stand on the sidewalk. I stare at the house opposite ours, which has been vacant for months.

It looks occupied, but I don't see a moving van or cars in the driveway.

Did they fly in?

Someone inside flips a switch, and a bright light streams through the open door.

"Jeena! Dinner is ready. Where are you?" I hear my mother call, but I don't turn back.

Winter is setting in. It is also getting dark, and I am alone on the street.

The cold settled in my heart makes me wrap my arms— it is only forty degrees, and not windy either. Anyway, I like cold weather. It is in my genes, my father said—his genes. He instilled a pride in me, in my physical ability to withstand any storm, any snow, any hail, any wind, any hazard that Nature might bring my way.

So, this shivering, this unusual tremble, this blocked chest is not about the cold outside.

I continue to stand and look.

The open door is a magnet of possibilities. Its promises entrance me.

■ ■ ■

One month back, I wouldn't even have noticed, let alone cared about an open door.

But it's different now. I am different. Dad is gone, and he has left me frozen inside. Dad never taught me that cold can come from within. He only taught me how to brave the Nature outside.

His heart had never felt alone, atilt, or adrift.

The open door radiates a hope that beckons.

What sort of people leave their front door open so anyone can walk in? How long will they leave it open?

It is unusual in America for a front door to be wide open, late in the evening, where the custom seems to be doors that are closed. If I walk up to a house, ring the doorbell, and someone opens the door, I already know, though I cannot see this, that they have inspected me through the piece of glass set in the door somewhere at adult eye level, high above my head.

"Jeena, stand away from the door when you ring the doorbell, far enough for them to see you," Mom has instructed me, because in my excitement, often I forget and lean into the door—as if to teleport myself through.

It's not only front doors that are closed. When I go for a sleepover to my friend Anna's house, she closes the door to her room so her mom and dad can't walk in or look at us as we play.

"Why do you close the door, Anna?" I used to ask. "We are not doing anything that your parents can't see."

"No, Jeena. We need our privacy," Anna would say with an assurance I wished I had. "And they don't want to hear our noises, anyway."

Anna is my best friend, and we giggle and whisper though we can be as loud as we want because of the closed door.

I notice that Anna's parents close their bedroom door too. Anna's elder sister is in high school, and she keeps her door closed when she is in there. Her door has a handwritten piece of paper taped on that says, *Keep Out.*

It is different in my house. Mom and Dad did not close their door, and I was not allowed to close mine. They said privacy is not about closing a door. Even at night, they left their door open. I remember crawling into their bed, right in between them. They didn't mind, and I loved it. We went into one another's room whenever we wanted. We didn't close inside doors except to go to the bathroom. In fair weather, or on weekends when we were home, even the front door was left open. "It's good for cross ventilation." At night, or when out, we closed it and then we looked the same as others in the neighborhood.

Houses in America are designed so doors can be closed without affecting access to common areas. A typical home has a corridor with rooms going off on one or both sides so each person can close the door behind them. "Just like a hotel," Mom says. "What is the point of having a house, a home, a family if we shut ourselves off in our rooms?" She doesn't subscribe to American notions around security or privacy. "What is the privacy for? You need privacy from strangers or when you shower and change clothes, but why do you need privacy to lie in bed and read a book? Listen to music?"

Dad was born in Michigan, but he agreed and said we had nothing to hide from one another. Open doors must have been customary where Mom grew up in India because Mom is a pretty private person in other ways. For example, Mom and Dad didn't kiss in public as I have seen other parents do. The most they did was hold hands when they thought no one was looking. Dad sometimes sneaked a peck on Mom's cheek, and she blushed red in spite of her dark skin. It was almost a game they played, their own secret game. Mom's ideas about privacy are her own, and Dad loved her just the way she is. And I loved my dad best and saw her only through his eyes.

So, I don't admit it to anyone, but on Saturday afternoons, when we were home together, when I was in my room, I wanted my door open. The soft breeze that wafted through our house carried sounds that connected our family and made us special. It was as if an invisible thread wove through our bodies—fine yet strong in a flexibility that allowed us to be independent without being unsociable. I could hear the clattering of Mom's utensils in the kitchen, my dog Zeena's snoring in the yard, and Dad practicing his music on the living room piano. We had a bond in our family that withstood distance, separation, and the cold.

I close my eyes and recall his music. An open door reminds me of us—as a family. It helps me summon the inner warmth that binds us.

■ ■ ■

I remember the man who visited us last month when Dad was on a trip. He knocked on our door and when Mom opened it, he asked, "Are you Mrs. Maya Mann?" and when she said, "Yes, I am," he said, "May I come in?" The man wore a dark suit and carried a briefcase. He was from the State Department. He showed identification and asked to sit in the living room. He said he would not be long. When he saw me, he asked to meet with Mom alone, but she said it was fine for me to be there. If she had known what was coming, she might have agreed with him, but with Mom, I don't always understand how she thinks.

"Mrs. Mann, I am sorry to have to do this, but I must inform you that Mr. Jerald Mann's vehicle was ambushed in

Pakistan yesterday. He was traveling to a remote village. It was a routine assignment—security inspections and audits. We had no warning that he was in any danger. It was unexpected, and we have initiated an inquiry."

"How can that be? He called me yesterday."

The man took official papers out of his briefcase and handed them to her.

"I am sorry, Mrs. Mann."

He let himself out the door, and Mom sat unmoving, staring at the papers. I don't think she remembered I was still sitting there.

After the man left, I sobbed, pummeled her body to get a reaction, and threw a tantrum.

"How could he? How could Dad die and leave us alone?"

Mom seemed to come out of shock and held me tight. "Shh," she said. "Shh."

She was not crying.

I did not understand. "Is he gone? Gone-forever gone?"

She nodded and crumpled the papers to the floor. Still no tears. In my rage and confusion, I turned on her.

"You! It's your fault. You didn't love him. If you did, you would have stopped him from going to dangerous places. I hate you." I thrashed out of her embrace.

I said a lot more. I don't recall how long I ranted. Along with my grief, hurtful words poured out uncontrolled; how I had never seen her display affection publicly; how she wouldn't stop him from going away. She said Dad's job brought him fulfillment. She knew it was unsafe, but she had no right to stop him. She said their love was sacred but private.

What about me? Did she even love me?

She sat in place till I calmed down. Then I ran to my room and slammed my door shut. She did not follow me or knock on the door. I realized my mistake and opened the door, but the moment had passed.

At night, I heard her sobbing herself to sleep. Every night. Night after night. She needed me but I did not know how to help. I froze when I thought about a future without Dad.

Last night, I found the courage to crawl into her bed and hold her tight. It started the thaw. She talked. She told me that while she had thought about returning to India, she had now decided America was our home.

"Would you prefer that, Jeena?" she asked. "I want what is best for you. Jeena, you are my reason for living now." Then she held my face in her hand, looked me in the eye, and said my outburst was healthy. That I shouldn't feel bad about what I had said. She was glad I could express my anger, sense of betrayal, and feelings of loss. "Dad loved you very much, Jeena. And he loved me too. He loved us enough to last seven lifetimes." That's what she said—it's the Indian in her. And she told me what she meant by seven lifetimes.

"Your dad will always be with you. He lives inside and around. What you have to do is close your eyes and call him."

And that's how I can hear Dad practicing the piano. Even though he is dead.

■ ■ ■

But when I am with Anna, when she comes to my house for a sleepover or to do homework, I close my bedroom door because I understand it's the American way and I want to be an American. Mom doesn't say anything about it.

There is no contradiction in my mind. So what if Anna's habits differ from mine? She is her own person and so am I. I look like Dad except I have Mom's dark hair, and his hair was gold. I know this because sometimes when strangers assume I'm white, I don't correct them. When they call me Jane, I let it go, though I am proud of my name. Dad said small slipups don't reflect the true person. Mom said I am American whether I am brown or white.

They are both right.

But since Dad died, such little things make me anxious.

That is why the open door has me transfixed. It is the door to our new neighbors. They must have moved in during the day when I was in school. If I walked into the bright, warm kitchen, what would happen?

Who are these people? Will they welcome me or will they think I am strange to visit uninvited?

I drop my arms, square my shoulders, take three deep breaths, and ready myself to face the world. I march up the driveway, to the front door.

"Hello. Anybody home?" I yell as I press the doorbell on the wall.

I am not cold anymore.

20

WHEN MOMS GROW UP

What difference does it make to the dead, the orphans and the homeless, whether the mad destruction is wrought in the name of totalitarianism or the holy name of liberty or democracy?

—Mohandas K. Gandhi, *Non-Violence in Peace and War*, 1948

Matt and Jeena were classmates. I met Mrs. Morrison for the first time when she came to drop off Matt for Jeena's fifth birthday party. She rang the doorbell.

"Hello there."

I recognized Matt from the playground, where he would usually play with Jeena, until I picked her up from daycare. I bent and hugged him welcome. Matt ran in without ado, right past me into the backyard, leaving behind on the porch the woman whose finger he had held seconds earlier and a toddler.

"I am Matt's mom, and this is his brother Mike."

I saw a tiny woman, impeccable in a flowered dress with big hair and no visible makeup, standing erect. She picked up the chubby two-year-old in her arms so we would be at eye level for the introductions. Mike took a soggy fist out of his mouth and waved. Both were happy as can be.

"Can we stay too?" she asked with a smile.

"Of course. I would love that. I am Maya, Jeena's mom, as you might have guessed already."

She put down Matt's brother and held his hand, and we walked inside. Mike looked up at me with eyes luminous and curious. One plump palm circled firmly around his mommy's manicured finger. I remember noting that his look was fearless, and in that, I thought he looked very much like his brother. They lived down the block and had walked over.

As was customary in those days, I had invited Jeena's entire prekindergarten class along with the moms, who were welcome to stay if they wanted. But so far, Mrs. Morrison was the first and, as it turned out, the only mom who stayed.

From that first moment at the door, we formed a connection. I found she was a lawyer after she confided, "You know, as much as possible when I am not working, I like to spend time with Matt and Mike. They grow up so fast."

"I am the same way," I said.

And we bonded over the hard choice we had made, balancing work and family priorities and the difficulty of getting quality daycare.

Sleep? What's that? We sympathized. We fretted about the ache of having to leave a sick child at home to attend an unavoidable work commitment. We joked about *quality time* as experts were telling us those days. In that, our first meeting, her so very American self-confidence and friendliness instilled in me a love for all people in my new adopted country. She transformed America from merely a land of opportunity to a land of good people. That was twenty-five years ago.

Our children grew older and changed schools and activities, and as their schedules changed, they drifted apart. Mrs. Morrison and I met less frequently too. Life moved on. In due course, we lost touch, and even though we lived in the same neighborhood, I did not see her for many years.

Today was Memorial Day, and I saw Mrs. Morrison on the front page of the *San Jose Mercury News*. Her small frame had stiffened shoulders to bear the burden of the Stars and Stripes that was hanging in colorful glory behind her. I had heard about Matt and grieved an impersonal grief at that time. The caption said she was a Gold Star Honoree. She had addressed a gathering at the function. That must be why she was on the cover page.

It was such a surprise. I could not stop staring at the paper. Her wild curls were still beautifully frizzy. Her tiny frame was still as erect and as proud as I remember it. But there was red color on her lips. It looked like a gash across her mouth. She never wore lipstick, I remembered. The picture was grainy, so I narrowed my eyes, held the paper closer, and looked again. *Where is the smiling woman with the booming voice that belied her tiny frame? Where is the wide-open smile?*

What I saw was a tear on her cheek. Grief had aged Mrs. Morrison like time never could. *Is that it?* I tried, but I could not see that mom who transformed me from an alien to an American.

I read the article. Now I was reminded of my mother. My grief had turned personal. I saw images of two medals, side by side, that were captioned:

> *The Gold Star Lapel Button (left) is presented to the families of service members who lose their lives while engaged in action against an enemy of the United States. The Next-of-Kin of Deceased Personnel Lapel Button (right) honors those who lose their lives while serving on active duty or while assigned in a Reserve or National Guard unit in a drill status. They are normally presented to eligible family members prior to the military funeral service. They are not meant as awards, but as symbols of honor.*

Award? Honor? Are we playing with words or lives?

I didn't read anything in the article that acknowledged what had changed Mrs. Morrison so utterly and what had aged her beyond her years. *The pins are designed to signify the loss of a loved one in support of the nation.* It seemed that the public, like me, didn't know about this honor because the article quoted one Donna Engeman:

> It's heartbreaking to think that a mom wearing a Gold Star might have someone ask her, "What a beautiful pin! Where do I get one?"

Donna Engeman is a Gold Star wife who manages the Survivor Outreach Services program for the army.

Yes, it was an honor, but not one Mrs. Morrison opted for. It was not her choice. Mrs. Morrison did not opt to be on the front page of the newspaper on Memorial Day. She accepted the honor, because what other choice did she have?

It was Matt's choice to join the army. Matt grew up tall and intense. He collected medals, awards, and honors, and then one day, he was killed. Today was the annual memorial in San Jose where over 1,500 people attended the service honoring area Gold Stars. *Does it say fifty families? How many Gold Star honorees? How many moms? How many mothers?* I couldn't remember. The number grew every year.

Mine was one such mother. Her son, my brother, had joined the Indian Air Force, and when he was twenty-one years old, his plane crashed while on a solo combat flight. My mother went to his air base in Hyderabad to bear the burden of his bravery and came back home with the Indian tricolor. She stood stoic and expressionless while they folded the flag into her arms with great pomp and a multi-gun salute. She appeared on the front page of the local paper, and Mrs. Morrison, on the front page of the newspaper today, looked like she did then.

When she later came to live with me in America, I found that my mother, who taught me how to be brave, could not attend a funeral, any funeral, or memorial. She would not have attended a Gold Star memorial ceremony. *Did she have the steel I see in Mrs. Morrison's back?* I wonder.

She must have. Or how else, as an alien in America, could she have showered unconditional love on Jeena, Matt, and other friends? She loved birthday parties. And it was not only children she opened her heart to. Her enthusiasm for the seniors in her Los Altos Seniors Sewing Club was unmatched. She shopped, gardened, and attended weddings. All day, she smiled and looked beautiful. How could she have done that if she let her lacerations show?

Only I knew that, sometimes at night, she got nightmares and would wake up screaming. I would hold her until the paroxysms passed. There was nothing to say.

I wished I could hold Mrs. Morrison today or do something to help her. It would help me too. I had nothing to say to her. I wondered if she had those nights when she had paroxysms.

I wonder, *When do we go from being moms when all we had to do was love our children to becoming mothers who hold up the sky?*

I thought about my mother, myself, and all moms who must grow up and become mothers. Moms who make the hard choices, and mothers who have hard choices made for them.

21

GARDEN OF PEOPLE

*The fish in the water is silent, the animal on the
earth is noisy, the bird in the air is singing.
But Man has in him the silence of the sea, the
noise of the earth and the music of the air.*

—Rabindranath Tagore, *Stray Birds*, 1916

"Papa, is *native* a bad word?" I ask softly, half hoping the urge
to ask would go away.

My father leans his tall frame over the balustrade. He is
inspecting his garden to make sure that plants needing protec-
tion have been tended to. Each one has a small, dried bamboo-
leaf thatch roof supported on sticks that traps the night dew
and prevents moisture from getting into the leaves where it
can freeze. There is a chill in the evening air. Tonight, the

temperatures are expected to dip. An overnight frost is long enough to kill his delicate new seedlings.

I grasp the importance of his job and why he concentrates so much, and perhaps that is why I have chosen this moment to ask my question. I had blurted the only sentence that came to mind.

I stand on my tippy-toes, bolstered by my elbows with my chin resting on a flat surface of the low wall, staring at the garden. I am preoccupied with feelings that clang inside my head. Thoughts jumble themselves up until I don't know what to say, but the urge to question does not pass. With effort, I marshal my words, enough only to voice the same query again.

"Is *native* a bad word, Papa?" I ask, louder this time.

The wall overlooks a sunken garden with symmetrical flower beds, tall trees, and short shrubs. Even as a toddler, I took a keen interest in digging, mulching, weeding, watering, planting, feeding, and all manner of care that my father lavishes on his garden. He has taught me the name of every flower. There are foreign ones: calendula, sweet peas, tulips, and larkspur, along with Indian varieties of chameli, gainda, and gulab. I can classify what blooms when. I am proud because I can identify a plant just by looking at the shape of its leaves. He has taught me to study the different categories of root systems, so I know how to prepare the soil for a plant even if its foliage is foreign. Despite different attributes, I can name a plant's lineage and family to decide conditions for its nurture.

I go with him on his annual winter trips to nurseries to buy exotic plants that thrive in our cool climate in the foothills of the Great Himalaya Mountains that dominate our lush, valley landscape. I listen to the questions he asks master gardeners and find the answers fascinating. He learns, not only from experience but also by gathering information from experts. He wants facts. That is why I know he will be truthful in his reply. I wait.

He says, "I haven't seen you gardening of late. What's keeping you busy, Maya?"

"I don't have time anymore." I pout. "I am reading to improve my English. Remember, you asked me to check out library books, and so I did."

In addition to Dickens, Shakespeare, and classics in our curriculum, I have discovered new writers. So far I have read every title by an author called H. Rider Haggard. *King Solomon's Mines* and *She* are my favorites. And I am reading Rudyard Kipling now. Their powerful imagery transports me into thrilling escapades in foreign lands, but occasionally I would be jolted from this imaginary world into my world because I could not relate to the subordinate status ascribed to local inhabitants by patronizing explorers.

"Adventure stories are the best, especially those set in Africa and India. I enjoy English literature now, but sometimes I don't understand what they mean when they write *native*," I continue.

"I see," he says. "Did something happen?"

"Somewhere I read *bloody native*. It seemed nasty. Or is it only a description?"

He waits a while and then adds, "*Native* is not a bad word. But first tell me, in this garden, which flower do you like best?"

■ ■ ■

His voice floats across fifty years and thousands of miles with the clarity of the sunshine that surrounds me. I am on the Stanford Dish, a small hillside preserve in Palo Alto, where every so often during my lunch break, I go for a walk alone or with coworkers. Today I am here because I signed up for the annual United Way Day of Service with a group of South Bay volunteers to restore the area to its natural habitat. My job is to clear out space, dig a hole, plant oak seedlings, and pull out the nonnative species overtaking the hillside. They are overcrowding the California scrub oak. I am told the nonnative plants suck up too much water and have ridden the hillside with squirrels. I learn from biologists about the flora and fauna in these foothills. I treasure this chance to be outdoors, but my heart weeps when I must pull out a healthy plant.

"I like them all, Papa," I remember saying. "A garden won't be pretty if we only had one type of flower."

"I think so too," he continues. "Native refers to a person, plant, or animal originating in a particular region. In this garden, plants come from all over the world so some are native while others are not. If left untended, plants can overgrow and choke one another so we weed and trim. Other times, we must help the plants from far away live in a different kind of soil, humidity, or temperature. With the right care, the plants adapt, and then they thrive together. When they do, our garden is prettier."

"Am I a native, Papa?" I persisted.

"Yes, you are, Maya. So am I. So is Mahmoud. Many of our friends and relatives have moved here from somewhere else. Meena Mausi moved here from Punjab. Mr. and Mrs. Roy moved from far away Bengal, where the weather is different. They had to learn a new language, eat new kinds of food, and wear different types of clothes. Still, they are classified as native because they are Indian. Your English teacher, Mr. Martyn, is from England, where the weather is much the same as here, but he is not native to India. However, he has lived here almost his whole life so you could say he has become native to the area, like Meena Mausi."

"So when someone calls you a *native*, is it good or bad?" I dog on.

"After some time, it is not possible to differentiate native plants from nonnatives irrespective of appearance. We grow a prettier garden. It is the same with people. *Native* does not imply good or bad. A garden of people living happily together is what we call a civilization."

I stomp away.

I remember thinking he does not understand the gravity of my question. But of course, he did. It was just that I was growing up too fast and he wanted another year of innocence from his child.

■ ■ ■

He fulfilled my curiosity with a literal answer, but he did not address the underlying question about judgement implied in the usage of *native* in books I was reading. I was too young to be satisfied with the greyness of his reply. I wanted answers in black and white. He was wiser. He knew that one day I would appreciate the image he had unfolded for me. And when needed, I would know how to act.

I relax. I sit back on my haunches, soak in the sun, and take a well-deserved break. I turn my head around to see my fellow gardeners. I recognize no one, yet the group camaraderie of individuals engaged in a common purpose is as physical as the benevolent sky above me. I reminiscence about my father's choice of words and rephrase. "Natives as well as immigrants flourish here." I live in a civilized country.

I believe I am obligated to preserve the character of my adopted country. Also I must fulfill this duty for my daughter's sake, who is born native but feels a foreigner in her own country. I must for my sake.

With my brown skin, I don't appear native to Palo Altans. However, I am home here and a foreigner in my native India, where my father and mother survived tumultuous years of colonial rule that culminated in an independent India in 1947 and where they died at peace with themselves and the world.

My colleagues, friends, and relatives share with me the dream of justice, equal opportunity, and fair play. My principles are reflected in the actions of individuals around me. But now I worry that the people I know are but a small slice of America, and so on this hillside today, I am acutely aware of changing political climes. And I reflect that maybe it is changing my behavior for the worse.

The other day, mistaken for a Latina at the grocery store, I was rude. "I bet I've lived here longer than you," I said.

Recent migrants to California who have not seen persons with my features set in brown skin often err this way. Usually I smile to prevent awkwardness as I tell them I am from India.

Yesterday I snapped. Perhaps because I confused a friendly overture for insolence? I cannot allow that behavior. It is honest to acknowledge differences; indeed it is the essential step before discovering similarities.

I am a first-generation immigrant from India and easily mistaken for Hispanic or Native American. Unlike India, where races have intermingled for ages, America is young and curious about where we came from. DNA studies offer no conclusive proof, but there is enough evidence to show that the earliest settlers came here in boats on rising tides. Or they travelled across the Aleutian Islands from Siberia and parts of Asia, further south. The current popularity of software applications identifying ancestry and the easy availability of DNA-typing tests is another indication of our collective obsession with race and origins.

We know we come from all over. I want an America where we care and create community, where we smile at strangers on our lunch break walks. I respect the land I have adopted, and I rationalize. And so must the strangers around me.

I raise my head and look up into the sky until the sun warms my skin. Bright as the clear sky, content as the companionship of gardeners, a feeling grows within my heart. My garden of people will prosper if I express love, understanding, and trust. Whether I am mistaken for a native or a foreigner, I am here to flourish. Whether they believe I belong here or I should leave, whether they think they own the rights to the resources of this land and I do not, no matter what they reason, I must cultivate this garden.

I look at the stranger next to me and smile. "Aren't we lucky to be outdoors and have the opportunity to make new connections?" I introduce myself and shake hands, and we pause our work to admire the hillside. I marvel at the ease with which, despite differences, we have found common ground.

I plant a seedling, pat down the soil to cover and nurture its roots, and promise to do my part in this civilization called America.

"Thank you, Papa."

22

TRADITION

I, to the world am like a drop of water, that
in the ocean seeks another drop...

—William Shakespeare, *The Comedy of Errors*

The setting sun casts an orange glow over the grassy slope, the raised cement platform that serves as a stage, and the makeshift wooden rampart that serves to hide the actors from audience view when offstage. I take one swift glance at the hubbub around me as I look for a place for us to sit, and I have already time-shifted.

Given that it's a weekday, it is a minor miracle that we have made it to the park, let alone on time, equipped with low chairs, a picnic basket, and adequately chilled wine. *Is it a minor miracle or the tenacity of tradition?*

"How's this spot, Jeena?" Mark walks ahead. He beckons and smiles. He knows how important this evening is to me, and he wants it to go well.

"Perfect." I love him for understanding. It is, after all, my mother and my tradition. And now, I hope, mine and Mark's.

We settle down. A trumpet announces the start of the program. A hush falls in the open-air theatre. The *Comedy of Errors* begins with a flourish from the fools. I clap. Everyone claps.

I am ten again. Yet I am also fifty. I see no dichotomy in being in two spaces so far apart in time. I am in the moment now as well as then. An evening in the park ameliorates my angst today as it did forty years ago when I attended Shakespeare in the Park with my mother. She started this tradition after Dad, the artistic one in our family, died.

Even though I was too young to comprehend the subtleties in the dialogue, without fail, at least once every summer she took me to see a play performed by a semiprofessional local or touring company. When she watched the play, the person she loved most, Dad, was with her. I saw that in the quietude that enveloped her normally hyperactive persona, though she said she started the tradition for my edification. She said that it wasn't only about the play. It was about the players too, striving against odds, keeping the spirit alive. Young as I was, I knew what she meant.

It's tradition. An evening in the park with the Bard is exactly what I need. Now I am here with Mark, and my mother is somewhere in the blades of grass beside us. I love being in the shade of tall trees and feel the evening breeze as it fans across all of us. It unites us today as it did so many years ago.

My anticipation of the lines, the slow smile that moves across my face, my wonder at the artistry of the performers, and my awe at the mystery unfolding before me are the same as before, even though now I know the story.

I hear every line like water drops. Yes, we are drops seeking other drops. But this evening, I am more. I am a drop that travels in time to find itself wondrous again, carried on a wave of words—effortless, seamless, and ageless. It matters not that I know the ending. I journey again.

When the play ends and the hat is passed, I drop a generous amount in it and know that I can never repay the debt I owe the players in my life. A father who taught me the power in artistry and joyfulness and a mother who kept his love alive long after he was gone made me who I am. And the actors today enabled me to immerse myself in the wonder of worlds alien to mine.

We get up and gather our belongings. I hug Mark. I am rejuvenated. For how else could I be so happy sitting on poky grass, drinking now-quite-warm wine, and eating cold food? Why do I not notice that the lighting is less than perfect and that my aging ears don't hear all the words before they float away in the wind?

GLOSSARY

(Adapted from Wikipedia: https://www.wikipedia.org/)

Almirah - Indian English. A wardrobe, cabinet, or cupboard. Typically, it is not built-in but added to a room like furniture.

Ashram – A hermitage, monastic community, or other place of religious retreat for Hindus. Ashram first appeared in English in the early 1900s and gained traction after Indian leader Mahatma Gandhi founded his famous ashrams at Sabarmati near Ahmadabad and at Sevagram near Wardha. The word *ashram* derives from a Sanskrit word, "srama," which means "religious exertion." Later in the 20th century, English speakers broadened the term "ashram" to encompass any sort of religious retreat, regardless of denomination. In addition to practicing yoga and meditation, a devotee may also receive instruction from a religious teacher and do some type of manual or mental work during her stay at the ashram.

Amma – Hindi. Word for mother, like Mom.

Belpatra – Literally means leaf of Bel (wood apple). It is offered in prayer rituals especially to Shiva. This leaf is trifoliate which signifies the holy Trinity: Brahma, Vishnu and Shiva. Read more at: https://www.boldsky.com/yoga-spirituality/faith-mysticism/2013/importance-of-belpatra-bilva-leaves-036354.html

Burka - A long, loose garment, usually black, covering the whole body from head to feet, worn in public by many Muslim women. Also spelt burkha, bourkha, burqa, burqua.

Chawl – Marathi. Housing units in chawls are rented by relatively poor but employed families. Historically chawls were constructed during the early 1900s in Mumbai to provide cost-effective housing to textile mill-workers and later built by working-class people in other areas. This type of housing is still in demand because of relatively affordable rents. Chawl residents usually have a greater sense of community than is implied by the words slum, or tenement.

Dhaba - A roadside restaurant or cafe. These are found on highways and on the outskirts of cities, towns, and villages. Initially started by enterprising Punjabis to cater to the needs of truckers, for authentic wholesome, clean, and hot food. They typically offer 24/7 service. At night some dhabas will replace tables with string cots along with simple bedding for overnight use. Dhabas are now a common feature on national and state highways. Earlier frequented only by truck drivers, today eating at a dhaba—urban or roadside—is a trend and has become a part of the culture of India.

Diya – Hindi. A small oil lamp made from baked clay. Used for prayer, or ceremonial occasions.

Dupatta – Hindi or Punjabi. A length of material worn as a scarf or head covering, typically with a salwar- kurta outfit, by women from South Asia. A dupatta is traditionally worn across both shoulders in the front and drapes in the back.

Ghat – Hindi. A series of steps leading down to a body of water, particularly a holy river. Used by bathers to reach the water. The set of stairs can lead down to something as small as a pond or as large as a major river. The numerous significant ghats along the Ganges are known generally as the Varanasi ghats and the 'ghats of the Ganges'. Some say these were constructed under the patronage of Maratha rulers such as Ahilyabai Holkar in the 18th century - https://en.wikipedia.org/wiki/Ghat#cite_note-2 – while others say they have been there in one form or another since historical times since Varanasi is considered the (arguably) oldest, living, modern city.

Kholi – A housing unit of one room usually situated in a chawl.

Kurta – A loose, typically collarless, knee length shirt worn by men and women from South Asia. Fashion designers nowadays make kurtas in all shapes, lengths and styles for women. The term Kameez may also be used interchangeably with Kurta.

Lorry – Indo-British. A large, heavy motor vehicle for transporting goods or troops; a truck. Synonym: big-rig or eighteen-wheeler, pickup truck or van.

Monsoon - In India and nearby lands, the season during which the southwest monsoon blows, commonly marked by heavy rains; rainy season.

Namaste – Hindi. A respectful greeting common in India. It is used both for salutation and valediction. Namaste is usually spoken with a slight bow and hands pressed together, palms touching and fingers pointing upwards, thumbs close to the chest. Sometimes spoken as Namaskar, Namaskaram in the Sanskrit form.

Papa – Sometimes used in India for father, like Dad.

Palloo – Cloth that drapes over the shoulder. It is part of the garment worn by women in India. See Sari.

Raja (or Maharaja) – King (or great king) historically. On the eve of independence in 1947, India (including present day Pakistan & Bangladesh) contained more than 600 princely states, each with its own native ruler, often styled Raja or Rana or Thakur (if the ruler were Hindu) or Nawab (if he were Muslim). The British directly ruled two thirds of India; the rest was under indirect rule by the princes under the influence of British representatives. After independence most Rajas were either given respectable positions (Governorship of their State) or became politicians.

Sari – Hindi. A garment worn by women from the Indian subcontinent. It is a cloth drape varying from five to nine yards (4.5 meters to 8 meters) in length and two to four feet (60 cm to 1.20 m) in breadth that is typically wrapped around the waist (tucked into an undergarment called petticoat), with one end draped over the shoulder, called Palloo, covering the breasts. It is worn with an upper garment usually called Blouse or Choli. Saris can be very expensive or low-priced and the cloth can vary from silk to cotton or muslin and nowadays nylon.

Swami - A Hindu ascetic or religious teacher

Sweetmeat - An item of confectionery or sweet food. Indian type dessert.

Vibhuti – Sanskrit. Sacred ash. It is a grey powder used in holy rituals by priests. It is the ash formed by burning wood (often mango) and Camphor and can be bought by devotees along with other offerings for prayer.

ABOUT THE AUTHOR

Writer, technologist, and unabashed geek Neerja Raman did research at universities, programmed at small start-ups, and worked as a manager at large corporations. She received her MS in chemistry from SUNY Stony Brook and her MSc from Delhi University. Raman has been inducted into the Women in Technology International Hall of Fame.

Raman's short fiction has been published in various periodicals, and she received an honorable mention in the Katha Fiction Contest (2017) for her short story "Garden of People." She is also the author of short essays and other nonfiction, as well as *The Practice and Philosophy of Decision Making: A Seven Step Spiritual Guide*, available on Amazon.

Raman is a distinguished visiting scholar at Stanford University. She is an avid hiker and can often be found gardening, advocating for women in STEM, or being politically and socially active in women-empowerment groups.